Emily and Penny Sue are sisters who grew up with the love of animals and writing. Painting and playing piano are a favorite pastime of theirs; they also ride horses on the side. Among many armature stories, one rose to the top. This is when they wrote there first book at the ages 14 and 15. They currently live on a farm in Kentucky with their family, two dogs, three cats, and their horse.

To Bree, Z, Renna, Dar, and Moniqua for being the best
friends in the world!

Penny Sue Seago and
Emily Seago

M.A.X.X.

AUSTIN MACAULEY PUBLISHERS™

LONDON • CAMBRIDGE • NEW YORK • SHARJAH

Ordering Information
Quantity sales: Special discounts are available on quantity purchases by corporations, associations, and others. For details, contact the publisher at the address below.

Publisher's Cataloging-in-Publication data
Seago, Penny Sue and Seago, Emily
M.A.X.X.

ISBN 9798889104698 (Paperback)
ISBN 9798889104704 (Hardback)
ISBN 9798889104728 (ePub e-book)
ISBN 9798889104711 (Audiobook)

Library of Congress Control Number: 2023918286

www.austinmacauley.com/us

First Published 2024
Austin Macauley Publishers LLC
40 Wall Street, 33rd Floor, Suite 3302
New York, NY 10005
USA

mail-usa@austinmacauley.com
+1 (646) 5125767

Special thanks to all the Kentucky folk who gave two new authors a chance, without them, *M.A.X.X.* would never have been.

Prologue

"Let me tell you a story that I have lived through. This story has affected me and will continue to affect me for the rest of my life, and I hope it will affect you too. Shh! Now don't interrupt because, in order to understand this story, you have to pay close attention to every element and twist. Wait! Before I start, I want to remind everyone to brush their teeth and get settled down and comfortable. Okay, so listen to every detail and get ready for some nonstop action in a story I like to call…'M.A.X.X.'"

Chapter One

12:02 a.m. November, Tuesday 12, 2047

FBI, CIA, NASA, IMF, SNOW.
Technology wipeout. Reason unknown.
Come immediately!
—SNOW

Marie Winterfield saw her airmail, quickly put on skinny blue jeans and coat, and grabbed her white rabbit fur purse.

As she whizzed down the road at 130 miles an hour in her razor-blue Import car, she called her father who was the head of the FBI.

"What happened out there?" she asked, still a little sleepy. Her dad's holographic, mole-rat-like face appeared out of the projector on the console of her car.

Captain Kernel answered his daughter, "We have no idea. Everything just shut down at exactly 12:01 a.m. Our best men are in the room searching for clues right now, but they aren't having much luck so far."

Marie was confused, "You mean someone was in the room? How did he pass security?"

Kernel answered, "Don't know, but it was all short-circuited. Even with our advanced technology, it's almost impossible to trace. Whoever did this was no amateur like the technology idiots we have trying to figure this thing out." Kernel made a disgruntled face and said, "Everyone is here, including the CIA, you better hurry."

"I'm two minutes away," she said, almost flooring it.

She ended the call, and her dad's bald face faded back into the console.

The SNOW headquarters was a madhouse as light flurries of snow came down outside the window. Agencies from all over came to see what happened to the main electronic and technology systems. The blackout originated from the main office of the SNOW building, which was Marie's office since she was the head of the SNOW operation.

As she reeled to a stop on the front parking lot of the SNOW building, she couldn't help but notice how the air was chilly and small flurries of snow fell. She looked up at 'her' building. She felt an overwhelming sense of pride as she gazed up at the magnificent structure thirty floors up. Fitted with the most lavish lobbies and stunning office views, not to mention the most advanced technological security system ever made before.

Then how could this happen? she thought.

Marie headed in at an alarming rate; she made note of all the people, who were obviously from different agencies, who were just loitering in the lobby. Some had worried looks on their faces, and some looked mad, while others seemed to be the happiest people in the world: smelling the flowers, staring at the water fountain, and one guy even seemed to be fascinated with the floor, which happened to be LED light-up crystal.

As Marie rushed up the stairs and down the hall, it was unusually quiet. The only noise that could be heard was the 'clip-clop' of her high heels on the cut-glass floor. She enters her office, where Kernel is scanning a spot on the desk with his Scan-Phone.

"Anything?" Marie asked hopefully.

"I think I found a fingerprint here," Kernel said pointing to his Scan-Phone.

She walked up and watched his phone. The fingerprint showed up on the screen.

"Yes!" they both whispered, a wide grin creeping across each of their faces.

Kernel chuckled, "At least this guy makes mistakes."

Suddenly, instead of the phone showing any identity information, it said only one thing, M.A.X.X.

Marie cocked her head. "What's a M.A.X.X.?"

Kernel was staring intently at his screen.

Marie looked up; her green eyes filled with tears, "It's all my fault, Dad. I should have put in better security. I should have known better."

Kernel put his boney hand on her shoulder, "Marie, you have the best security system in the world. There's no way to get a better one."

Marie slammed her fist on the desk. "Then how is this possible? There's not a single clue as to how this guy got into my system. Or even who this guy is! Except for the word M.A.X.X."

She felt a buzz in her pocket that stopped her from speaking. She pulled out her phone and looked at the screen. What she saw jolted her into action. It showed big red numbers that began to count down: TEN...NINE...EIGHT...

She yelled, "Get everyone out of the building! Dad, hit the alarm!"

She ran into the bathroom and threw her phone into the toilet. That had been protocol. Since the new phones that came out shut down the moment, they hit sewage water.

As soon as she got outside, where everyone else was, the roof of the building burst up with a wave of brown water, and a fountain rained down on everyone.

Marie gasped and gagged, along with everybody else who was standing around, and she regretted throwing her phone away immediately. The bitter cold of winter was now accompanied by stale, dank air that smelled like an outhouse.

Marie could see through the windows of her precious building as all the electricity went out. A part of her heart broke when she saw what she had worked all her life for being reduced to nothing but a glorified sewage pipe. Another tear streamed down her face.

Throughout town in the distance, other explosions could be heard.

Immediately, Marie, her dad, and the others got in their Import cars and sped down the road. Throughout the city, the sewers burst out of the ground; fountains of brown sewage water ran all through the city's streets, along with an extreme power outage.

Marie stopped her car, hopped out, and stood next to her dad.

Kernel said in awe, "Man, this guy's good."

Marie pulled her spare phone out of her pocket and dialed 911.

"Nine-one-one; what's your emergency?" the operator answered.

"Yes, I would like to report a bomb," Marie said. Suddenly, a piercing, screeching noise came from the phone's speaker. Marie threw the phone to the ground just before it burst into flames.

Her dad looked with his jaw dropped and said, "Wow, this guy is really, really good."

Chapter Two

Wednesday, Thursday 14, 2047, 12:01 a.m.

Marie answered her phone, "This is Marie."

A shaky voice responded, "H-h-hi. Um, is this the police?"

"What is your emergency?" she said seriously. Though she was not the police, she did need to know if this was associated with the case.

The youngish voice said, "Hi, I got a call a few minutes ago, and it was like a threatening voice. He calls himself Maxx. Anyway, I think you should come down and, you know, check the place for fingerprints or investigate or whatever it is you guys do. This isn't a trap…by the way."

The line hung up. Marie instantly called her dad, "Dad, we have to go."

The boy who called was sitting on his couch eating a cookie. It had been three minutes since he called what he thought was the police lady, and he was proud of himself.

When a knock sounded at the door, he took his sweet time to answer it, but when he did, Marie went straight to business, "What is your name, kid?"

The boy said confidently, "Jason Plumber, mam."

Marie looked him over, and her eyes narrowed, "How old are you? And where are your parents?" The boy had dark hair that was on his face and a marker mustache.

The boy gasped, "I am a grown man, thank you very much…thirty-no, twenty to be exact."

"Twenty?" Sargent Kernel chortled. "I wouldn't be surprised if you weren't a day over thirteen."

Marie got them back on track, "Did you have any physical contact with this…Maxx?"

Jason shrugged, "Nope. Didn't see him at all."

Kernel demanded, "What did he say to you?"

Jason put his head up and thought for a minute, "He called me, and I think he said something like, 'Jason Plumber, you have been activated. Now listen carefully to the following instructions because I won't repeat it again…'"

Marie asked, "What were the instructions?"

Jason had a perplexed look on his face, "I can't remember."

Kernel got very annoyed and yelled, "Give me your phone!"

Jason dug threw his pockets franticly, then finally pulled it out, and handed it to Kernel.

He opened it, and after a bit of searching, he was able to pull up all the recent phone calls, "Here it is."

Marie leaned in close as Kernel pressed the play button. The voice that they heard wasn't disguised or muffled; in fact, it was perfectly clear and precise. The man that was talking wasn't hiding anything; he said it in the most casual voice as if he was telling his best friend or younger sibling.

The voice said, "Yo, Jason, your gonna be activated. Listen carefully to the following instructions because I really don't want to repeat them."

The rest of the message was gone.

Twin gasps escaped Marie and Kernel.

Kernel's face was so red he resembled a cherry (a moldy cherry), "What? No! It's deleted! The rest is deleted!"

Marie looked bewildered; then she looked at Jason, "Did you delete this recording?"

Jason had a far-off look, "I don't remember."

Marie narrowed her eyebrows and looked at her dad who turned to Jason.

"Did you eat or drink anything since the phone call?" Kernel said pulling out a flashlight and shinning it into Jason's eyes.

Jason nodded and happily held up a cookie, "Yeah, I had some Girl Scout Cookies. Some girls sold them to me today."

He turned around and handed them the case of cookies.

Marie looked closely at them and sniffed, "These cookies are coated in Daylight Powder. It makes you lose all recent, important memories."

Immediately, Marie and Kernel turned and walked out of the house.

Kernel ordered one of his men, "Track down those Girl Scouts; we are gonna make an appointment."

Marie looked at her dad, "It doesn't make sense; if he wanted Jason to go somewhere, why would he erase his memory?"

Kernel said, "The message was for us. He is playing with our heads like a cat with a…well, whatever a cat would be playing with."

Marie got in her car and followed her dad to the Girl Scouts.

"I don't know anything about him. All I know is that he called me on my phone and said that I had better sell these Daylight cookies to some kid, or else he would tell my parents all my secrets."

Kernal and Marie were asking each Girl Scout their side of the story.

"He called me on my phone and said if I do this he would give me a hundred bucks."

Kernel asked, "And did he give you a hundred bucks?"

The black-haired girl responded delightfully, "Yup."

"Did you see him?"

She shook her head, "No, the money fell out of a tree."

Marie and Kernel sighed as they head back to the car.

Marie said, "A definite phone call from this same guy Maxx, but we still got nothing. How is this possible? I'm so confused. We don't even know what he looks like!"

Kernel said reassuringly, "Don't worry, Marie. People who toy with the system never make it far. We just need to keep searching."

Marie put her hand on her dad's shoulder, "I'm glad I get to do this with you, Dad. I don't think I could do this on my own."

Kernel said with a far-off look, "You are capable of more than you think, Marie. More than you think."

Marie didn't know what that meant then, but very soon, she would find out.

Chapter Three

Thursday, November 15, 2047, 12:01 a.m.

Captain Kernel twiddled with his fidget cube, running his thumb across a dial that clicked softly, while he sat at his desk, trying to figure out a solution.

Every lead seemed plausible at first but ended up being a dead end.

His lamp was the only light that lit the dark room. It casted an eerie gloom to the room. A noise jerked him out of his thoughts. It was coming from the doorway. A footstep? A gun clicked…He froze.

A shaky, unprofessional, child's voice demanded, "Don't move."

Kernel looked up at the kid with a gun in his hand. He held it with shaky hands. There was a second kid as well, an older girl, which looked like the kid's sister.

The girl rushed to Kernel's desk and opened a compartment. She started searching through it franticly, as the boy held the gun at Kernel. Kernel looked at the girl, who was closer to him, and noticed that she had an earpiece in.

The girl pulled out some top-secret files and examined the label. She said aloud, "Yeah, they're here. What do I do with them?"

An inaudible voice answered her from the earpiece. Kernel asked, trying to stall, "Did Maxx send you?"

The boy was shaking, but he held firm, as the girl took out a lighter and held it under the files until they lit on fire.

Kernel's bloodshot eyes widened, and he lost it, "No, you can't do that!" He jumped up and started yelling.

The kid with the gun demanded with a trembling voice, "Stop. Be quiet! Don't move!"

The voice from the kid's earpiece said, "Kill him."

The kid was trembling as he pointed the gun at Kernel. Kernel jumped up; the kid aimed; and the gunshot echoed throughout the city.

Marie was searching through files when her brand-new phone rang. She grabbed it, "Marie here."

What she heard on the other line made her go into panic mode.

She gasped, "What? How? I'll be right over."

She put her phone in her pocket, immediately ran out the door, and was at the FBI headquarters in a few minutes.

Marian, her employee and best friend, walked up, "We don't know how it happened. We did find fingerprints that led to a couple of kids, but the database shows that they were perfect kids until last night. He was shot down, and we found ashes of some very important irreplaceable documents. We will see if we can do anything with those."

He paused and looked at Marie's reddening face, "Do you think Maxx did this?"

Marie shrugged sadly.

Marian said emotionally, "I'm so sorry. You don't need to be here. You should take a few days off to grieve." Then he walked away.

Marie walked into her building, plugging her nose and avoiding the cleanup crew, and to her office where she could be alone. As her eyes started to water, she began to cry uncontrollably.

An APB was put out for Maxx, even though they had no idea who or where he was. Marie was determined more than ever to catch this criminal and make him pay for his crimes. The game was afoot.

Out on the street, about one mile away from the FBI building, stood a nineteen-year-old guy about 5'7", who called himself Maxx.

He flipped his dark, shaggy hair out of his face and looked up at the huge electronic images on the buildings, seeing an award for him.

This, he already knew, but this time, he saw the charges of…murder. Murder?

He didn't like that at all. This young genius was smart enough to know exactly what was up.

His face was perplexed; then it formed into a slight smile, sort of a small, mischievous grin (a grin that you will soon know as his signature smile).

Maxx had a plan, and he was about to execute it.

Marie was at HQ when the phone rang from her Scan-Phone. She looked at the screen and almost threw it across the room.

On the screen were big letters that said "M.A.X.X." and a picture of him. Dark brown hair, blue, blue eyes.

She yelled, "What the heck!" and she ordered, "Mr. Fulton, patch me through!" Marie swiped the button and put the phone to her ear, "Hello?"

"Hi, Marie, you might know me as Maxx."

Marie said, "How did you get this number? And how did you get your picture on my phone? That is your picture, right?"

Maxx said, "Look, Marie, I'm going to cut to the chase: I have something to tell you. Meet me exactly in the middle of Time Square, right in the middle of the street. Be there at exactly 12:01 p.m., I mean literally, 12:01. I'll be standing there for three seconds. If you aren't there within that time frame, I am leaving, and you have lost this chance forever."

Marie heard from the background, "Tell them about the cookies."

Maxx said to the voice, "Shut, just shut up, Jay! I'll get there."

Marie asked, "How are we supposed to meet in the busiest spot in the world?"

Maxx said smugly, "Figure it out. I want to see how much you really want me, and if you don't, I'll give you a reason to."

From the background, "You didn't tell them about the cookies."

Maxx sighed resentfully, "My baby brother wants me to ask you how you liked the cookies."

Marie looked behind her and saw Marian with a box of white-powdered cookies. His mouth was full, and he had one in his hand. His eyes widened, and he threw the box in the trash.

Maxx said, "You know what? Hearing myself say this out loud, it sounds really dumb. Let's just get back on point. Don't be late or early, and to you, FBI, CIA, and SNOW people who are listening in on our conversation: don't forget handcuffs because, in case this isn't clear, I'm turning myself in."

Marie had a confused look on her face.

Suddenly, all the cameras and TVs and huge screens lit up with Maxx's face. It was as if he had FaceTimed them, without them even answering.

Maxx said not to them but to someone out of the screen, "Man, I was so nervous. Do you think I did okay?"

Jason Plumber came into the picture, "Yeah, I think you covered all the parts."

Jason looked at the screen and narrowed his eyebrows, "Uh, Marc, I don't think you turned it off though."

Maxx picked up the phone, his face even on the ceiling and floor, and he said, "Remember, call me Maxx. What do you mean? I pressed the red button."

Jason said, "You pressed FaceTime."

Maxx looked at the screen and yelled, "Ahh! No, they'll discover all our secrets!"

Jason tried to soothe Maxx, "Just press the button."

The picture became a blur of motion.

"I am pressing it!" Maxx smashed the phone with his finger, "Stupid phone!"

Jason was trying to calm him down, "You're not doing it right. No, you got to clutch it!"

Maxx yelled outraged, "I'm clutching the stupid thing. Okay, I am!"

He yelled at the phone and threw it to the ground, where Jason picked it up delicately. The screens showed Jason's face as he waved a smile and hung up.

Marie stood there staring for a minute before growling, "Jason Plumber, the little rat, played us."

Marian popped up with a half-eaten cookie in his hand, "Do you think he is actually going to turn himself in?"

Marie shrugged her shoulders, "I don't know, but we can't miss this opportunity. Gather the teams! We're going to Times Square."

Marian ordered the men, "Gather all your gear, people. Let's take this guy in!"

A young, seventeen-year-old intern girl nervously looked at Marian because she knew something that everyone else did not.

Later on that day, Time Square was desolate. No cars drove by or honked; no angry New Yorkers yelled or cursed at each other. There could only be one explanation for why people would clear out so suddenly. Every luminous sign read: Possible COVID-19 virus in the area.

The people fled because everyone thought they knew the phantom dangers of COVID-19.

Marie, Marian, and all the rest of the undercover crew were hiding in different buildings, waiting for Maxx to reveal himself.

It was 12:00 p.m., and Marie was ready to walk. She turned to Marian and whispered, "Do not let anyone shoot him unless he is proven a threat. No one hurts him. You got it?"

Marian nodded and told all his associates on the walkie-talkie, "All units, do not fire on Maxx unless I say so."

In the shadows, Marie noticed a dark figure walking toward the center of the road.

She looked at her watch, 12:01.

She took a breath and looked at Marian, and he nodded.

She walked out into the center of the road, straight toward this shadow…Maxx.

She took in the look of this stranger; *He was definitely the man on the phone.* He was not at all disguised, but most shocking of all, he was barely an adult, possibly just turning twenty.

At twenty-five years, Marie was considered young to be in her kind of position. Compared to that, Maxx was just a kid!

He smirked, his dark hair looking black with the night. "Marie Winterfield, it's an honor to finally meet you."

Marie said in the firmest voice she could manage, "Enough with the formalities, Maxx. Did you say you have something to ask me?"

He did a full smile, all teeth included, "True, but I'm not that dumb. I would rather ask you when your whole team is not listening in on our conversation."

Marie was being honest, "We're always listening."

He lost his smile partially, "No, you aren't. Your agencies think you can see, hear, and smell everything about everyone, but the truth is that none of you know anything. You're not in control; you don't hear anything; you do not know anything; and anything you think you know is just a masquerade covering up the truth. I'm not just talking to you, Marie, but to everyone listening in on this conversation through your earpiece that sticks out so plainly. And this is not a threat; it's just the truth. So you might want to bring me in before you expect me to ask anything."

Marie looked down and sighed, "Okay, follow me."

She turned around and walked back toward Marian. Surprisingly, Maxx actually started following her, even though she figured that he would have a bigger plan than this.

As she approached Marian, she said, "Marian, put down that darn gun!"

Marian, who was pointing the gun at Maxx with a shaking hand, narrowed his eyebrows and put his gun down.

He spoke into his walkie-talkie, "All units, stand down. The suspect is now friendly."

Maxx had a satisfied, triumphant look on his face when Marian said that.

A couple of men walked out of the shadows, handcuffed Maxx, and shoved him into the back of a prepared van.

Marie watched with wonder, as they loaded this very young criminal mastermind into the back of the police van.

This young man seemed very calm and composed. She knew he had a plan, but one could never tell. He had a look on his face that already said, "I won."

Marie had a feeling deep inside that the journey was just beginning, and it would only get harder and harder.

There were many questions still unanswered for Marie. But she was determined to figure out the answers for each one, starting with 'Why was her father killed?' and 'Did Maxx really have anything to do with it?'

Chapter Four

Sunday, November 18, 2047, 3:08

The white-walled room consisted of a single table and two chairs.

Two men in their everyday black uniforms brought Maxx into this room where they handcuffed him to the table.

Marie looked through the glass at this criminal.

She took a breath and walked into the room. "Maxx, my name is Marie, now I will…"

Maxx interrupted, "Look Marie, I'm just going to cut to the chase. I didn't kill your father. I don't use kids like that except my baby brother. I just had to get that off my chest."

Marie raised her eyebrows. "Okay, about your brother…"

Maxx interrupted again, "Ah, nope, can't go there. I don't talk about my brother to you people. I came here to tell you the truth; I am trying to get seen so that I can use you for the plan that is wrapped up in here." He pointed to his head.

Marie asked, "And what would that be?"

He narrowed his eyes at her and then decided, "Nope, I can't trust you enough yet to tell you my secrets."

Marie was frustrated, "Why are you toying with the system?"

He gasped as if he were offended, "Mam, I would not call my work 'toying'."

Marie stayed on track, "Is it for money?"

He shook his head and looked down, disappointed at her.

Marie gasped slowly, "Oh, I see. It's something deeper, a story as old as time, revenge."

Maxx laughed a bit and looked up at her with an evil eye, "Smart girl. Ha, ha, no…" He suddenly got serious, "I don't know where you got that from."

Marie sighed, "What can you tell me?"

Maxx raised his eyebrows, "Well, I think for really anyone, it is the fact that you don't have to live within the boundaries that everyone else has set in the history of our time. You don't have to follow the rules."

Marie was disgusted at his saying, "Quite the opposite. You do need to follow the rules. Now, tell me something important about the case."

Maxx looked up and narrowed his eyes. Then he said, "Did I mention my name is Maxx?"

Marie slammed her fists on the table and said to everyone who was listening on the other side of the glass, "I can't break him!"

She stormed out of the room and walked into the lady's restroom.

Everyone outside heard an outraged scream escape her.

The guards who were watching the camera where Maxx was sitting looked at each other when they heard Marie scream.

No one had ever been able to make Marie this uptight. The two guards scrunched up their faces and looked back at their cameras, and Maxx was gone!

A bloodcurdling scream echoed through the whole building.

Marie ran out and saw the chaos. Marian was outraged, yelling at the officers who were watching Maxx. And Maxx…well, Maxx was nowhere to be seen.

Marie lost it. She ran up to the guards who were watching him and interrupted Marian's yelling, "What happened! You were supposed to watch him! That's all I said to do! How could you let this happen?" She gave them a very stern look. She turned around to conceal her discouragement; then she walked away.

The rest of the day was frustration for Marie. She was in her office all day long, searching files and listening to recordings of Maxx's interrogation.

Something didn't sit right with her. When she asked him to tell her something important about the case, he said, "Did I mention my name is Maxx."

She didn't know why this bothered her so much; something about this whole investigation was off. Ever since the start of this case, everything was off.

Then there was something else: something that she couldn't put her finger on something that actually did have to do with what Maxx said.

She leaned back in her chair and looked at the clock, 12:01 a.m. She decided to wait for 12:02 just in case anything might happen.

She thought about the case some more. What was it that bothered her so much? *Maxx said that he was trying to use her for the plan that was wrapped up in his head. What could that be?*

Nothing was clear now; she had to wait for more pieces.

It was 12:02 a.m. when she got up and announced to the guards, "I'm locking up for the night!"

She went out to her car and drove home.

At two o'clock in the morning, Marie was tossing and turning in her bed.

This case is making her restless. Her dad, the secret papers, Maxx, no.

She shook her head. *It's not right*, she thought to herself. *When we first saw the name Maxx, it wasn't Maxx. No, not at all. It was M.A.X.X.*

She leaped up in her bed and said aloud, "Maxx isn't the name; it's not his name at all! When he said, 'Did I 'mention' my name is Maxx?' that was actually a question. He never said his name was Maxx, ever! We all just assumed! Maxx was telling me something, trying to get a message through. A message that only I would get. But what was it?" She gasped, "I've gotta tell Dad!" she stopped herself with sudden realization…she was on her own now.

She got up and pulled out her X203000 laptop.

In the dark, she googled the letters "M.-A.-X.-X."

Many different websites popped up, but they were all the same: M.A.X.X. was an organization.

She immediately shut down her laptop.

She thought to herself, *This is dangerous. I need to get to my office.*

She headed out the door as soon as she grabbed her jacket and sped over to the SNOW building in her razor-blue Import car.

Technology and workmen, advanced as it was, had already started reconstruction after that whole sewage debacle.

She parked her car in the front and stepped inside the building. The crystal flooring was almost covering the entire floor, and the fountain was flowing (although Marie could almost swear that the watercolor wasn't as pure looking as it was before the explosion.)

Keith, the security guard, was at his desk sound asleep.

Marie woke him by slamming the desk, "No sleeping on the job! I could fire you for that!"

She walked past him and up the newly refurbished stairs, straight to her office where a Top-secret Compound Assistant Computer sat (to replace her old one with stickers and coffee stains). She sat at her desk. On this high-tech computer—that no one could hack into—no one could secretly see its contents except her. She punched in 'M.A.X.X'. Up came a super-secret organization, called the Mind Alternating 20 or, in other words, M.A.X.X.

Marie breathed as she read on:

Starting on July 20, 2020, M.A.X.X. was developed by Percy Owens Peterson, a young man who had the idea to alter the minds of children to make them change in ways that were unnatural. He chose twenty test subjects. Twenty kids were the beginning of this incredible idea. The children that were selected for these programs are on record for having incredible brain power, lightning quick movements, and being able to win any battle that they faced. Percy saw this as an advantage, and he used these children for 'law enforcement'.

In December, Percy was nominated 'Hero of New York City' because, with his child army, he lowered the rate of crime in the city by 88%!

However, two years later, the formula for the mind-altering child had negative effects as well. Some children were depressed; some needed periodic anger management; and some were physically damaged. It was found out that Percy had eliminated each one that had these disorders. Making it to where he had to have more kids. All over the world, public schools were raided, and all the children went missing. At first, thought to be an unrelated event, authorities finally found out that these missing children had been sent to the M.A.X.X. organization to become 'men and women'.

It was found out as well that giving a child the formula resulted in headaches, stomach pain, vomiting, muscle pains, and quite often death.

Percy tried to cover it up by setting the lab on fire, but the authorities got to the scene fast enough and were able to recover a good amount of evidence.

On August 8, 2023, 12:01 a.m., Percy Owens Peterson was arrested and later put to death for murder, kidnapping, child abuse, and arson. The M.A.X.X. organization was scattered and eventually shut down. The victimized kids have been recovered and rehabilitated. All other members of M.A.X.X. were found, or they went into hiding and are still out there. Although, going back into the history and data of M.A.X.X., some kids that were not killed were also not found or recovered. Families were devastated even more when they heard that their kids might still be out there. Because if they are still alive out there, then they are going to have it pretty hard...

Bursting with all this knowledge, Marie leaned back in her chair to think. This was a lot to take in; then it came to her, *What if Maxx is still part of M.A.X.X.? Or what if he is one of the unrecovered kids?*

Suddenly, she heard creaking outside her door.

"Who's there?" she turned off her computer and got up to look.

No one was in the lobby.

She heard honking outside, like in the parking lot.

She headed downstairs and looked out the window…nothing.

She told Keith, "I'm checking out."

She walked outside and immediately knew something was wrong.

There was a black car parked in the shadows, and it was running with the lights off.

She noticed that there was a person in a black mask and suit about 50 feet away.

She turned around to walk back into the building, but the doors wouldn't open.

Panic started to fill in her. Keith was gone.

She pulled on the door again, but it wouldn't budge. It was locked! *Darn it!*

The man in the mask started walking toward her. Marie turned and speed-walked in the direction of her car. She looked around and noticed that she was surrounded. People in black masks were everywhere, and they all started toward her.

She broke into a run toward her car, and all the others ran as well.

Right before she reached her door, a man in black jumped in front of her. She skidded to a stop and turned around, but she was surrounded.

Her heart was racing a million miles an hour, and she was so freaked out. She didn't even know why she wasn't screaming.

Suddenly, the most bizarre thing happened: all the fifteen vacant cars in the parking lot burst into life.

Their LED headlights were flashing; their horns were blaring; their engines were revving; and their doors were opening and slamming shut.

The whole parking lot was lit up like a football field in action.

It stunned Marie, as well as all the guys in black.

The noise was attracting all the guards from the SNOW building and everyone within a twenty-mile radius.

Suddenly, as if things weren't weird enough, with all the unoccupied cars coming to Marie's rescue, an enormous 2020 fashioned army tank burst through the few trees in its way and sped up to Marie and the men in black.

They all scattered, including Marie.

The tank skidded to a stop in front of Marie, and a man in a red mask opened the huge door and shouted, "Get in!"

Marie just looked at him doubtfully.

All the men in black masks saw the red-masked guy and ran toward Marie, in an attempt to take her one last time.

Suddenly, Marie was yanked into the tank, and the man in the red mask slammed the door.

The red masked guy stepped on the pedal, and the huge tank surprisingly lurched forward with a lot of speed.

All the guys on the outside jumped out of the way and got in their vehicles, ready to chase down the tank that was way over their height.

The chase was on.

The red-masked guy sped down the desolate road, with five black, tiny cars chasing it.

Marie was freaked out as she held onto her seat for her dear life.

The red-masked guy said, "Hang on."

Suddenly, he swerved the tank in a completely illegal U-turn and was heading straight back to the black cars.

Realizing their predicament, the guys driving the black cars swiveled around into another illegal U-turn, and the game was switched.

The red-masked guy was laughing hysterically as he was chasing the men in black down the road with his huge tank.

A couple miles down the road, the red-masked guy finally stopped.

The vehicles, that he was chasing, stopped and turned around.

The red-masked guy opened a small compartment in the tank, aimed, and pressed a red button.

Suddenly, the tank's gun on top started glowing red, ready to fire.

Immediately, all the black cars turned, sped away, and were out of sight within three seconds.

The red-masked guy laughed, "Works every time."

Marie looked at him with wild eyes, "That was crazy! What are you trying to do? Kill me?"

The guy said as if offended, "I just saved your life! Relax, Marie."

Marie stopped, "Wait, how do you know my name? Who are you?"

The guy took off the mask, flipped his dark hair to one side, and did his signature half-smile.

Chapter Five

Tuesday, November 20, 7:08 a.m.

Applebee's had a surprising special that day: onion rings with a pesto dip and grilled cheese chips with a side of green cheesy broccoli.

Marie thought it was the most disgusting food that Applebee's could have made, especially since the restaurant was outdated and should have been shut down years ago, or maybe changing it into a recycling plant would be better, considering the fact that all their food tasted like it had been recycled.

Maxx, on the other hand, happily ate his onion rings and cheese broccoli. He was so focused on his food that it seemed to Marie that he had forgotten she was there.

She sipped on her cup of unsweetened iced tea and waited for Maxx to be finished with his food because it didn't seem like a good idea to interrupt him.

Three minutes passed, and all of a sudden, Maxx looked at her and said, "I just wanted to tell you that Thursday is my birthday. Yep, turning twenty, maybe people won't treat me like a kid anymore."

Marie shifted in her seat, "Oh, that's good."

To herself, she was thinking, *He's not even twenty yet?*

Maxx said, "Yeah, I haven't had a real birthday since I was like…five."

Marie shifted again (this conversation seemed to be getting really personal).

She figured, *he brought it up*, so "Why?"

He gave her a sideways glance and, suddenly, got up and said, "I'll be right back."

Without hiding anything, he walked one complete circle around the table, examining Marie.

Then he sat back down, "Okay, I'll tell you. As I'm sure you figured out, my name is not Maxx; it's Marcos Alexander Plumber, and I am part of the M.A.X.X. organization—well, at least I was before I revolted and became a rebel."

Marie looked shocked, "What? That's impossible. That organization was dispersed long ago, way before your time. It's closed down now."

Maxx shook his head and rolled his eyes, "Marie, if you only look at the headlines and the cover of a book, you're never going to know the real story."

Marie looked at him and asked, "What can you tell me?"

Maxx settled in his seat and began to explain, "Well, I was taken or, as they put it, 'chosen for the program' when I was five years old. And, yes, M.A.X.X. is still operating, but it has changed over the years. They had multiple groups when I was there, thirty kids per group. I was in group number one, and they labeled me as, well, #1. They said that I had the most potential and that I was gonna save the world. But, first, they had to change me," as Maxx told this part, he was spacing out intently, remembering, "and they sure did change me.

"First, they brought us into a simple room and told us that we needed to be tested first. They made each of us from the group put blindfolds on, and they spun us around the same amount of our age. Then they made us sit down on a seat that I cannot explain. What came after that, I don't even know. They took the blindfold off of me, and I was the last one in the room. They said that I was the only one in that group who conquered the test. I was the only one in my group left.

"The next thing they did was take out a needle the length of a tent spike and said that it would elevate my performance skills. Being five years old, I didn't really know what they wanted me for. Anyway, they drove the needle down my arm and inserted me with the red liquid. It stung at first, but then within the hour, I got a massive headache. I can still remember the pain. That night was treacherous. But the upside was that the next morning, I felt like a new person, like I could do anything. Aren't these cheese chips amazing?"

Marie was caught off-guard by the question, but she noticed that the waitress was filling up their drinks.

Maxx smiled sweetly at the waitress, waiting patiently for her to leave.

The waitress smiled and stood there.

Maxx raised his eyebrows and shook his head to the left as in, 'Get out of here'.

The waitress gasped and walked away.

Maxx continued, "They taught me little, simple things for five whole years, and I succeeded. At ten years old, I was brought to Base16, which is where they kept all the kids that completed the tests. We were taught not to trust each other; we had no friends; we never spoke with each other; and all we knew were each other's numbers. The commanders taught us everything: technology, physiology, criminology, zoology, tomography, photography, human…ology…"

Marie interrupted, "That's not actually a—you know what, just keep going."

Maxx continued, "All those things, including how to read human thoughts. Not literally, but we could tell when someone was guilty, we could tell whether they hid the stash of money or not, by simple, tiny movements. The twitch of an eyebrow, the rubbing of hands, a quiver in their voice or movements. We could tell if they were hiding something or not. We were basically human lie detectors.

"We were always taught to look out for the best, to know when you are the best and when you're not. Which made me not that popular. I was literally the best in every one of those categories. I was the commander's pet. They told me in front of everyone that I would be the best and that I would lead them all.

"It even got to the point where they would give me normal, everyday clothes to wear, when all the others had to wear the same red uniforms. They said that I would be able to meet the great Percy Peterson, which was what everyone wanted to do, the founder of this organization, but no one saw him."

Marie stopped him, "Wait, Percy is still alive? They said he was executed years ago."

Maxx nodded his head, "One of life's great mysteries is how they get these broccoli florets so darn cheesy and juicy! Juicy and cheesy, weird combination, but it works."

Marie was frustrated, "How can you talk about broccoli at a time like this! We are at the brink of discovery and…"

While she was going on and on, Maxx said into his earpiece, "Jason, give me tabs on that waitress. She's looking at me weird."

Jason on the other line said, "Okay, just a minute, it's loading. Almost there, just a little, little bit more, and we are almost…"

Maxx was bored; then he stage-whispered, "Jason!"

Finally, Jason said, "Okay, her name is Mariah Hill. I mean Miriam Bill."

Maxx said to himself, "How can you misread that?"

Jason continued, "She is a—Oh, my gosh, she is FBI! Marc, get out of there."

Immediately, Maxx grabbed Marie's arm and said, "Let's fly!"

He yanked her up and dragged her away and then stopped.

He turned around and took out a $20 tip and set it neatly on the table.

Then, back to business, he grabbed Marie again and shoved her into the restroom.

Marie shook him off, "Look, buster, I'm not in the mood for any games!"

Maxx yelled over her in a voice that seemed to boom through the restaurant, "Will you shut up! You're blowing my cover, again!"

Marie was shocked and just stared.

Maxx went to a stall that said, *"OUT OF ORDER,"* leaned down to the toilet, and grabbed the whole bowl.

He said to Marie, "Here help me with this."

Then he started trying to lift the whole toilet off its axes. He was yelling at the top of his lungs, with effort, lifting the bowl. Marie could see sweat trickling down his forehead. Marie just watched and asked, "What are you doing?"

Suddenly, a stall door opened, and a little boy walked out and saw Maxx trying to rip the toilet off, with Marie just watching.

His only question was, "What is she doing here?" as he pointed at Marie.

Maxx said simply, "Because it would have been much weirder if I was in the lady's room."

The kid narrowed his eyebrows and said to Maxx, "And what are you doing?"

Maxx said with a smile, "I'm trying to take the toilet off, so we can escape the wrath of the FBI, CIA, and SNOW agents outside that door."

The kid gasped, "You're criminals."

Maxx said with a slight smile, "Well, kid, I'm afraid you know too much now."

He pulled out a gun and aimed.

The kid gasped, and Marie jumped up and grabbed the gun, "What! Don't shoot him, you crazy?"

Maxx looked at her, "It's a mild tranquilizer. He'll be fine."

Marie shook her head, "No!" She turned to the boy, "Kid, get out of here."

The kid ran away without another word.

Maxx returned to the toilet and tried to lift it, yelling at the top of his lungs. He told Marie, "Come, help me!"

Marie started to walk over when he suddenly laughed, "I'm kidding. It's easy."

He easily moved the toilet over with one hand.

Marie covered her nose, "Why aren't there any pipes?"

"I planned ahead."

She was looking down into the dark hole that reeked, an instant replay of the night that her SNOW building burst into stench with that phone bomb that Maxx had planted.

"You don't expect me to go down there, do you?"

Maxx sighed and looked down, "Yeah, it's never as bad as it looks."

Marie hesitated before Maxx grabbed her arm and pulled her in.

From down there, Maxx replaced the toilet.

Marie was holding her breath as they walk down the slimy tunnel.

One hour, or maybe it was two or three? Maybe longer.

They trudged through the slimy tunnels.

"Do you even know where we are?" Marie wheezed.

Maxx, who was ahead of her and hadn't spoken since they got in the tunnel, looked behind him with wide, shocked eyes, as if he had forgotten she was there.

Marie sighed in disgust, "Honestly, am I really that easy to forget?"

Maxx still said nothing.

Marie ran up beside him and noticed his face was green. He was holding his breath.

Marie ignored it, "Can we go up now?"

Maxx nodded his head and pointed up.

Marie looked up and saw a grate that led to the street.

Marie said, "We are in the sewer. Gross."

Maxx grabbed the ladder and started climbing up.

On the outside, the sewer grate was lifted out of place, and out came Maxx and Marie, smelling, well, like they just came from the sewer.

Night had already settled, and that was where Marie put her foot down, "That's it. I'm not following you anymore."

Maxx shrugged his shoulders, "Okay." He turned around and ran into the darkness.

Marie suddenly realized her predicament.

All of the sounds of the city came alive as she stood there, alone in the darkness.

The distant police sirens, angry men yelling at each other, tire screeches, gunshots, even babies crying.

Her eyes were wide, and she was getting very frightened.

"Maxx?" she looked into the darkness, where he had run to, "I know you're still there."

She stared silently, not a noise sounded from the darkness.

Her mind started to panic, "Oh, no. I'm alone out here, and I'm an accomplice to a criminal."

Suddenly, she heard running footsteps in the opposite direction.

She spun around quickly, to see one dark shadow running toward her.

Immediately, she turned and ran the other way.

Running out of pure adrenaline, she looked back and saw that the man was following her. She could tell off-hand that he was too tall to be Maxx.

She maneuvered a move that she thought was clever. She ran into a dark alley, where there was a dead end.

"Oh, no," she cried.

She turned around and heard the footsteps getting closer.

Then, right before her, the man ran around the corner and was coming straight at her.

Out of instinct, she whipped out her Mace pepper spray and lunged toward the guy, spraying it straight into the guy's eyes.

The man screamed in fear and dread, "Noooooo! My eyes, my beautiful eyes!"

Marie instantly recognized him. It was Marian!

She said as she put down the Mace, "Marian, what are you doing here, you idiot?"

He strained, with his hands covering his eyes, "I was about to ask you the same question. You've been gone all day! Ahhh!"

Marie decided not to tell him about Maxx, "I was investigating, undercover. The case."

He looked hurt, and it wasn't just because of his red eyes, "What? Without me? Did you find anything?"

Marie looked disappointed and shook her head, "Nope, not much."

Marian nodded his head and squeezed his eyes shut.

They stood there for an awkward second; then Marian said, "Well, what do you say I take you back home?"

She nodded, "Yes, that would be good."

As she followed him out, he was still holding his eyes, "I think you made me blind. Ahhh!"

She said, "Maybe we should hail a taxi."

She loaded up in a taxi with Marian, and they drove back to Marie's house.

In the darkness, watching them drive away was Maxx, who was there the entire time. He managed to keep up with them and stay hidden. Right now, he was doing his usual half-smile because he knew that he now had a lead.

His plan was playing out exactly as he had planned it.

46

Chapter Six

Wednesday, November 21, 2:00 p.m.

Marie walked into the FBI building and is shocked by what she sees.

A bunch of men were carrying all of her father's supplies, out of her dad's office.

Boxes were being moved, and chairs and desks were being hauled in and out.

Marie ran over and stopped one of the men who was carrying four boxes, "Hey! Who do you think you are doing? You can't take my father's stuff! Put these things back!"

The guy seemed innocent and tried to explain, "We have orders to relocate all these materials."

Marie demanded, "Orders from who?"

Suddenly, in her father's office, a man who was sitting in his chair swiveled around and said, "Me. I am Colonel Pop; I will be replacing your father. You must be Marie Winterfield, the daughter."

Marie scoffed, "What?"

Then Marian ran up behind and explained a little, "Marie, I tried to stop them from removing your dad's things, but I'm simply not in charge here. They brought Colonel Pop here for replacement."

Marie looked down and was serious, "No, I mean, it's okay. It's not up to me whether they get a replacement or not. I'll go and get some coffee."

She turned and walked out sadly.

In the lobby, as she was sitting, she thought about this M.A.X.X. organization.

Maxx said that Percy Peterson was still alive. If so, then why was Maxx here? He said he revolted and escaped. Which meant the whole organization was after him. He also said he had a plan, in his first interrogation.

She thought to herself, *Maxx must be planning to take down the whole organization, but how?*

Suddenly, it dawned on her, *He's looking for Percy Peterson, the guy that started it all.*

Marie narrowed her eyebrows, *He's never seen Peterson before, but Peterson had indeed seen him.*

This she knew because she recalled reading that Percy kept tabs on every one of his subjects, and if Maxx was indeed the best, then Percy for sure knew what he looked like.

Yet she knew that Maxx already knew that, but something still bothered her. She felt the presence of something or someone who wanted Maxx for a dark purpose. She knew that she had to keep her meetings with Maxx secret because someone in this very building was hunting Maxx not for the purpose of interrogation. She could feel it.

But she knew that she needed Maxx also. She needed not only to bring him in but also to keep him safe.

In this way, she felt completely responsible for his safety. He was only a kid after all.

A voice spooked her out of her thoughts, "Ma'am?"

Marie jumped and looked at the one who was speaking to her.

It was the young, seventeen-year-old girl, who was Marie's associate. Well, technically, this girl wasn't actually even part of SNOW. She just helped out a bit.

Marie answered her, "What is it, Ann?"

Ann said, "Um, this was left on your desk for you." She held out an envelope.

Marie took it and thanked her as Ann walked away.

Marie opened it and read the paper silently.

"What is it?" Ann asked standing on the balls of her feet to read over Marie's shoulder.

"It is a notice stating that the late Captain Kernel's position in the FBI has been replaced by Colonel Pop former head of the CIA." Marie was saddened by the overwhelming need for her father. Suddenly, an alarm sounded throughout the whole building.

She jumped up and stuffed the envelope in her pocket.

All the agents were rushing out the door in a great hurry.

Marie grabbed one of their arms and demanded, "What's going on?"

The guy said, "An order was just passed out to all the agents! We are to go out and find Maxx in any way possible and take him out anyway necessary! No one got any breaks until he is in our custody or dead!"

Marie was horrified, "Who gave the order?"

The man said quickly, "The new manager." Then he shook her off and ran out.

Marie stood there and stared for a second before rushing to Colonel Pop's office.

His office was super busy; people on computers; men and women were rushing around with papers; and Pop was at his desk writing franticly.

Marie stormed to his desk and slammed it with her fists, "Why did you pass out this order? This is not standard procedure!"

Pop said, unhindered by her anger, "Standard procedure never seemed to work when your father was in office, so now I am the colonel, and we are going to take this little twerp down once and for all."

Marie insisted, "You won't find him. What do you think we have been doing for the past two weeks!"

Pop chuckled and said, "We've located his brother. When we have Jason, Maxx will come to us."

Marie was disgusted, "You're not gonna hurt his little brother! He had nothing to do with this!"

Pop said, "On the contrary, his brother is very vital to Maxx's whole operation. Evidence shows that Jason works most of the online technology. So we take Jason, and Maxx will come."

Marie seethed, "You don't think he'll have a plan? When you take his little brother, you don't think that he knows what he's doing."

Pop chuckled, "Oh no. we figured he would come, and trust me, we'll be waiting."

Marie took a step back and was at a loss for words.

Then behind her, she heard someone clear his throat.

She turned around and saw Marian all dressed in army wear.

Marie said, "What are you doing Marian?"

Marian seemed sad, and he looked at the ground and said, "Well, I have been put on the job of leading the group to take Maxx out."

Marie turned to Colonel Pop and said, "No! Marian is my agent!"

Pop spouted, "He had been promoted to FBI."

Marie was horrified, "You can't do that! He's part of SNOW!"

Pop said simply, "Well, just to remind you, Marie, the FBI had a higher ranking than SNOW ever will. We can do whatever we want. Including kicking you out of my office."

He waved his hand, and a guard man took Marie by her arm and started walking her out.

Pop said to her as they took her out, "Oh, and that alliance that the FBI and SNOW had when your dad was alive, well, that died with him. Thank you for your service. We do not need you anymore. The FBI will take care of this Maxx case from here on out. Bye."

The door slammed in her face as she stood outside in the hall.

She turned around, shocked at what she heard. Her father's agency was now split with hers. Now it was just her leading the agency, alone.

Maybe in another time frame, this would be her happy moment, SNOW was now completely hers, but this was more than that. She was taken off the case. This was impossible; she was stuck on this case. She had to solve it, with or without help from the FBI.

She walked out to her car and sat in the front seat. She took a deep breath and then pulled out of the parking lot.

Chapter Seven

Wednesday, November 21, 8:00 p.m.

The FBI interrogation room was much more rugged than the SNOW interrogation room. Downstairs, in the lobby, marches in Marie. A security guard tried to stop her, but she flashed her badge at him.

She headed straight upstairs to the interrogation room.

When Marian saw her there, his eyes widened, and he walked to her, "You shouldn't be here."

Marie informed him, "I have the right to attend any interrogation that I seem fit. According to the law."

Marian made a complex face, "Really?"

She passed him, to let him mule over that a little bit.

Suddenly, five FBI men came in dragging Jason Plumber.

Jason did not seem perturbed at all, and Marie was amazed at how much this kid acted like his brother.

Even now, he seemed to say, "I already won."

Marian walked up to the men and said, "Put him in the room. I'll be interrogating him."

As Jason sat on the seat, he twiddled with his thumbs until Marian walked in.

Marie watched from the window.

Marian said to Jason, "So, Jason, I know you know stuff about the agency and my former boss. Tell me what you know and have learned."

Jason stated in a Russian accent, "Well, I've learned that beauty is only skin deep, and actually, it's kind of beautiful what she is."

Marian had his eyebrows narrowed, "Oookay, tell me about your brother, Maxx."

Jason had a perplexed look by this question, "I don't recall, having a brother by that name. Nope."

Marian was losing patience easily.

Suddenly, over the PA, a female voice announced, "Marian Cogsdale, Colonel Pop wishes to see you in his office immediately."

Marian got up and said to Jason, "We're not done."

Jason quickly said, "My brother will come for me."

Marian turned around and smiled, "We're counting on it." He walked out.

Marie stood there at the window, watching Jason.

She thought to herself, *"I wish I could help him out of there."*

Suddenly, someone appeared in the interrogation room. A face that Marie totally expected to see but not like this.

In the interrogation room, next to Jason, was Maxx.

Maxx grabbed Jason by his arm and yanked him to his feet. He glanced over at Marie and put a small, folded paper under the table, all the while staring at her as if to say, "I am putting this here. For your eyes only."

Then, just like that, he brought Jason to the door of the interrogation room, opened it, and was gone.

The alarm sounded suddenly, and the room was in chaos.

Both Maxx and Jason were gone.

Marie couldn't believe her eyes.

But that was because her eyes deceived her, for in reality, what Maxx did was this…

After he put the note under the table, he grabbed Jason's arm and pulled him toward the door as he said, "Jason, how many times have I told you to be careful? I'm not always gonna be able to watch over your stupid head!"

He opened the door completely, making enough room to block Jason and him from anyone's view. Then super quickly, he opened the small air vent that was situated right at the door. Suddenly, he stopped and saw 'her'.

A girl who looked seventeen, Ann, in fact, was staring right at him!

For a split second, his mind yelled at him, "You're caught! Panic!"

But then he looked into her eyes and saw that she wasn't like the rest of them.

Yet her hand was lifted up, ready to sound the alarm that was right next to her.

He shook his head no.

She looked into his eyes and slowly started to move her hand away.

As soon as she does, Maxx grabbed Jason and throws him down the air vent.

At that, Ann lifted her hand again, but this time, Maxx didn't wait. He jumped down the vent, quickly replacing the lid to the vent, and Ann slapped the big red alarm. And the alarm sounded throughout the building.

The door slowly shuts.

All this happened within the time frame of five seconds.

Marie jumped up and ran over to the door.

Marian and Pop ran onto the scene and saw Jason gone.

"Where did he go?"

Pop was outrageous.

Marie noticed Ann, who probably sounded the alarm, which means that she saw them.

But Marie didn't want to tell Pop that, or he might interrogate her. Ann worked for Marie, and Marie needed that.

As Marie looked back at the empty scene, where Jason and Maxx were one minute before, and she couldn't help smiling, as she admired Maxx's handiwork.

She turned around and said to Ann, "You're Ann, right? I want you to come with me. You're gonna take Marian's job and follow me around."

She gave her a notebook and a pen, "You are to write down everything you see, hear, know, and even smell. You turn it into me every night. And make sure no one sees it." Marie whispered, "It is a secret."

Ann smiled and nodded. She was happy about the promotion.

Marie looked at the table with the folded paper under it.

She didn't forget it.

Chapter Eight

Thursday, November 22, 9:29 a.m.

That morning, Marie surprised herself with where she was, a New York shopping mall. It was a pain to get there with the snow. It was coming down almost constantly now, yet she found herself birthday shopping as you could say.

Even though what she was looking for was completely related to her business.

Ann was right at her side, scribbling something in her notebook.

Marie was in the hair section of this particular store.

She figured to herself before she met Maxx at the library; she would get him a present and a disguise.

She picked up plenty of hair stuff, super expensive hair stuff, and bought it.

In her Import car, she told Ann, "Can you wrap these up really quick?"

Ann grabbed all the hair and disguise stuff and got busy.

Marie was right at the library when she saw three black cars parked in the back, standing out with the snowy background.

They were the same ones from that car chase at the SNOW building.

She stopped her car and watched.

The guys in the black cars saw her and just stared for a second.

She stared back; suddenly, the black car burst into action and sped forward at Marie.

Immediately, Marie did a doughnut, struggling to keep her car from spinning out of control, and sped away in the opposite direction.

The car chase was on. Chase two…

Ann looked behind them and was already at the heart of the matter, "They're gaining on us! Speed up!"

Marie was literally flooring it, "I am!"

Suddenly, out of nowhere, Maxx jumped up from the very back seat and said casually, "Mind if I save your life?"

Ann gasped as Marie did a blood-curdling scream.

Maxx was smiling, then said seriously, "You might want to hang on."

Suddenly, their car was slammed from behind causing them to spin and land in a ditch.

Marie looked back and saw that they were surrounded by black cars.

Maxx said, "Give me the wheel!"

Marie let go and said, "It's all yours."

Maxx jumped in the driver's seat, grabbed the wheel, and turned on the radio.

A booming hip-hop melody emanated from the car as Marie squeezed herself onto the rider's seat.

Then, with Maxx at the wheel, Marie's little vehicle burst into life.

Their car sped forward out of the ditch, and away from the black cars that were trying to block them. Suddenly,

Maxx slammed on the break, and their car skidded to a stop, without sliding, making the black car behind them smash into their back.

Then Maxx sped left and down an alley, and two black cars follow.

The cars behind them were big, while Marie's car was small; the black cars were fast, while Marie's car actually had a speedometer. The odds were stacked against them one hundred to one, and Maxx was loving it, especially the fact that there was ice on the road. Every moment, he was in the zone!

Maxx maneuvered the car into a smaller alley, where the big cars couldn't fit.

The black cars tried to skid to a stop in front of the alleyway but kept going, smashing into a big blue dumpster, the black car behind him smashing into him blocking the alleyway.

Maxx sped super-fast through the alley and into open space. Suddenly, he turned the wheel super hard, letting the ice aid his drift, until he was facing the alley again.

Marie and Ann were horrified, and both yelled simultaneously, "What are you doing?"

Maxx did not answer as their little car sped back down the small alley toward the big black car that was in the way.

The man that was driving that car realized his predicament and jumped out of his vehicle, right before Marie's little car side-slammed the big car. Marie's car was so small, and the black cars were so big that Marie's car's hood easily slipped under the black car, and the black car flipped once and slammed into the wall behind it.

Marie was surprised at the effect and even more surprised that her little car was still running.

Maxx sped down the alley and into the busy street. He knew the other black car in the alley couldn't get out because the one he crashed was majorly in the way.

So Maxx sped down the road to get as far away from that scene as possible.

One hour later, Maxx pulled under a bridge and parked the car.

He leaned back in the driver's seat, deeply satisfied with himself, "Smooth as butter."

Marie finally yelled as she got out of the car, "My car! You destroyed my car! This is going to cost so much money in damage repairs!"

Maxx got out and looked at the car as if he just noticed its predicament, "Oops. Sorry."

Marie took a deep breath and hyperventilated a couple of times, her hard breaths coming out as fog in the frosty air before getting cheery again, "Oh well. Maxx, I wanted to tell you that I think some of your M.A.X.X. people are disguising as FBI agents."

Maxx nodded his head, "Oh yeah. I knew that."

Marie was smiling as she said, "And so I remembered that today is your birthday, so, since you are turning twenty, I got you this present."

Ann walked out of the car and brought up a poorly wrapped present.

She said, "Sorry, the car chase sort of banged it up a little bit."

All the while, Maxx was looking at it with such a feeling. He was touched.

He picked it up and said quietly, "You remembered."

Then he smiled and brought it to a nearby rock and sat down to open it.

He ripped off the paper and saw the many different hair styling equipment and different disguise stuff.

Marie and Ann were smiling as they watched his reaction.

He gasped as he looked at them, "Oh, wow, this is the stuff I always wanted. Thank you, guys, so much. Let's use it now!"

He stood up and brought them under the bridge.

Marie said, "Now?"

He nodded, "What better time than now? We might all be dead tomorrow." He started getting teary-eyed, then said, "You guys are going to have to help me though. Because I don't have a mirror."

Marie looked at Ann who nodded, "Of course, we'll help."

He smiled and said, "Okay, make me look like a different person. This is gonna be so awesome."

Marie and Ann smiled and got to work right there under the bridge.

About two hours passed before Marie and Ann stood back to take a look.

Maxx was sitting in anticipation, "Well? How do I look?"

Ann smiled silently, blushing, as Marie said, "Man, you look older. Take a look."

Marie took out her makeup compact, with her frozen fingers and pulled out a mirror.

Maxx looked into it and gasped. "I love it! Man, I got to do this more often. I don't even recognize myself." He laughed, "I bet you even Marian wouldn't be able to recognize me." His long, once shaggy dark brown hair was now trimmed, side-swept, and a German blond.

Miles away, in the office of the FBI building, on a dark night, a dark man waits, with a dark purpose.

Colonel Pop sat at his desk and summoned Marian to his office, "Marian, I want you to post agents all around Marie's house and wait for her. She's hiding something. I know it."

"That is actually illegal, she is a government agent." Marian protested.

"Just do it!" Pop seethed.

Marian sighed and looked down, "Yes, sir." He turned and walked out.

Pop sat at his desk with a far-off look on his face, "I'm gonna find you, Maxx. Yeah, you made your first mistake."

Pop chuckled a bit as lightning struck in his evil head.

Marie was in her busted-up vehicle driving back to her house in the snow, Ann sleeping in the back seat next to Maxx.

Suddenly, Maxx stopped Marie and said, "Stop! See that vehicle; those guys are watching your house. We should go somewhere else."

Marie looked at the vehicle parked at her house. It was the FBI.

"Oh! That impertinent, little—" Marie was muttering under her breath.

Maxx said, "You guys can come to my place; trust me, it's safe."

Ann woke up and said, "I can't." She laughed, "Marian might get suspicious if I'm not home."

Marie turned around and said as she carefully drove away, careful to stay out of the sight of the FBI car, "We can go to the FBI building, to drop Ann off with Marian. I'll stay at your place Maxx."

The FBI building was dark and barely lit, as Marie drove up to the front.

There in the doorway was Marian waiting.

Ann left her notebook in the car, jumped out, and ran up to Marian, "I'm here."

Marian walked up to the driver's side window and said to Marie, "Hey, I'm sorry about this whole Pop thing. I wish I could do something."

Marie nodded, "Yeah, me too."

Marian noticed the gentleman in the back seat, who had dark sunglasses on at night.

Marian said suspiciously, "Who's he?"

Marie said as casually as possible, "Oh, he was on the street, and I was giving him a lift to his home right after I drop off Ann. He's blind." She whispered the last part.

The man smiled and said in a very strong German accent, "Yeah, but I'm not deaf! Hello, sir. Good to meet you." He turned to Marie, "*Danka*, mam, for your hospitality."

Marian could tell that this man was born a German. His accent was completely unfakable.

Marian said still skeptical, "Yeah, nice to meet you too, mister…"

The German man said, "The name's Marc."

Marian nodded, "Ah, yes."

Marian said to Marie, "Be safe. I don't like the looks of him. Street people are dirty."

Marie nodded, "You all need to learn a little kindness."

She drove away into the darkness before Marian could say anything about 'Marc'.

Marian and Ann just watched as they drove away.

Marian turned to Ann, "What the heck happened to her car?"

Ann just looked down and loaded up in Marian's green Import car.

Marian and Ann drove home.

Ann looked at her brother in disgust, as he drove.

She said, "I know what you did, I know what you are."

Marian sighed and said, "Really, we're gonna do this now!"

Ann kept on going, "Why do you need Marie's agency separate? Does she threaten you or something?"

Marian looked at Ann with a sideways glance, "How do you know that?"

Ann crossed her arms, "I saw you and Pop talking. That's not all I know."

Marian's eyes were wide, "What else?"

Ann said casually, "Enough. I've been living in that house for years; of course, I would know. Did you think I was stupid that I wouldn't find out?"

Marian quietly said, "Marie cannot know. You had better not blow my cover."

Ann narrowed her eyebrows, "What cover, M.A.X.X.?"

Marian screeched the car to a stop, sliding a short distance before stopping and told her sincerely, "Don't ever repeat that name again if you want to live. Besides, that is behind me."

"No, it isn't." she challenged.

"Shut up, Ann!" Marian yelled.

Ann sat back in her seat and crossed her arms, "Fine."

Then she mumbled, "I wish mom and dad could see you now. They'd be ashamed."

Marian started up the car and gave his sister a sideways glance. He never understood how his little sister knew so much. He didn't care much about Ann; she was adopted, and someday, she might stick her nose a little too far into his business.

Jason Plumber was working on his high-tech computer system when a knock sounded at the door.

"What's the password, even though I know it's you, Marc?"

Maxx said from the other side, "Jason, I hope you cleaned the place like I told you to. We have a guest."

Jason fell off his chair, "Oh. Of course, I cleaned! I always clean."

He started cleaning and hiding stuff as fast as he could.

Maxx said mischievously, "Really, then can you let us in."

Jason picked up the remains of a hamburger and threw it across the room, "Of course. One second!"

He ran to the door and opened it, seeing Maxx and Marie, he said, "Hello, Marie! What a pleasure. Come in! Cleaned the place specially for you."

Marie walked in before Maxx and looked around.

It seemed like a comfortable home, but there were electronics, high-tech computers, old-fashioned laptops, and every other kind of technology.

She gasped, "Wow. You guys really have an advanced system here."

Jason said, "Yeah, we have all the work. Oh, this room is where all the hacking got done…"

Maxx elbow jabbed him in the gut. Jason laughed off the pain but shut up.

Marie sat on a couch and yawned.

Maxx said, "Oh, yes. You're probably tired. In fact, Jason, you should be getting to bed now, too."

Jason sighed and walked off down the hallway.

Marie smiled and said, "So this is where you've been hiding."

Maxx narrowed his eyebrows, "Maybe. Maybe not. This could very well be a trick."

Marie shifted in her seat and something crunched underneath her.

She held still with wide eyes and said, "What the heck. Maxx, something is under my seat."

Maxx said, "Stand up."

She jumped up and looked…there sat a crushed taco.

Maxx had a pained expression on his face, and he let his head drop back, "Ugh, Jason, he has such a stupid head."

Marie laughed.

Maxx said, "Yeah, time for bed. You can sleep in here."

He leads her into a different room with a bed, nightstand, and a lamp.

"It's nothing fancy, but it's home," he said looking around the room, checking to see if Jason left a half-eaten ice cream cone under the pillow.

She sat on a bed and said, "It's very nice."

Maxx nodded and walked out.

Marie took out Ann's notebook and opened it and read:

Today, Thursday, November 22

I had the pleasure of witnessing Maxx's great escape with Jason today. It wasn't anything fancy, believe it or not, he simply did things quickly. Well, him being part of the M.A.X.X. organization is kind of expected. I let him escape then pressed the alarm. Marie had assigned this job to me, which I'm not sure is a good idea, because of the fact that Marian is my brother. Though I do appreciate the promotion.

Three guys in black cars were chasing us down the freeway today. I got a pretty good look at them, and I could tell that they were from M.A.X.X. There is only one type of car that had a shiny black paint job and at the end of a horrible car chase, not have a scratch on them, including the one that Maxx turned over.

Plus, there is only one type of driving that drives like that as if the vehicles were alive and followed the driver's every command.

Take it from Maxx's driving; as soon as he had the wheel, the car came to life. These men were from the M.A.X.X. organization.

The vehicles were called, M.A.X.X. Cars. I don't know why, but the organization had a thing about naming their best items after the organization, like Maxx himself.

Today was Maxx's birthday; he turned twenty; and we gave him a present, hair stuff that would change his look. I feel so happy for him. It is weird, how I always feel happy when Marie and Maxx are with me. I don't care that they have made me an associate of a crime; when we are together, it feels like family. They are my true family.

Marie put the notebook down, a little teary-eyed. She was about to burst into tears of affection for this girl when she heard the commotion in the kitchen.

"What! How did you do that?"

It was a lot of chatter.

She got up and went to the kitchen where Jason was holding a tray with a tilted birthday cake.

She gasped and smiled, "Why wasn't I invited to the party?"

Maxx groaned, "It's not a party."

Jason was really proud of his cake, "I made it myself."

Maxx was sarcastic, "Really? No kidding."

Jason held it out to him, "Make a wish."

Maxx sighed and rolled/closed his eyes.

Marie and Jason smiled at each other before watching Maxx.

Maxx finally blew out all the candles in one blow.

Marie and Jason both started clapping.

Jason asked, "What did you wish?"

Maxx shook his head, "I wish…to go to bed."

He turned around and headed to his room.

Jason called after him, "I'll eat your cake then."

Marie looked at Jason and asked, "Is he usually in this kind of mood."

Jason shook his head, "No. It's only on his birthday. Fifteen years ago, on this day, he was taken away from me, mom, and dad."

Marie gasped, "He was taken on his birthday. How awful?"

Jason nodded, "I try to comfort him and make him forget about it, but there's not going to be any making him forget anything."

Marie looked in the direction of where Maxx went. Suddenly, she felt extra sorry for this kid. Most twenty-year olds are in collage looking forward to their future, but Maxx was still trying to fix his past. The past was ruined by this Percy guy. He never had a childhood.

She got a sense of determination right there. She would find this Percy and make him pay for his crimes, for the lives of many innocent children that he ruined one of which was Maxx.

She turned and went back to her room with a sense of triumph.

Jason sat in the kitchen and said to himself, "I guess I'll have the cake, then."

He looked down at the messy blob of cake and said to it, "I worked so hard on it though."

Chapter Nine

Saturday, November 24, 4:00 p.m.

Marie sat at her newly replaced office desk, thinking.

She had been sitting there for about an hour; suddenly, she jumped up, "That's it."

She pointed to Ann, who was sitting at her one assistance desk in the corner writing in her notebook, "Ann, how fast can you contact Maxx, wherever he is."

Ann stood up, "Immediately."

Marie nodded, "Good. You go to the Beaverdale Café and tell him to meet you there. I will be there shortly once I meet with someone."

Ann nodded then narrowed her eyebrows, "Wait, who?"

Marie said lamely, "Nobody."

Ann nodded and picked up the phone on her desk and dialed a number.

Marie was looking at her with narrowed eyebrows.

The phone answered, and Ann gave it to Marie, "He's on the other line."

Marie was impressed, and she picked up the phone, "Hi, Maxx, this is Marie."

On the other line was a strange robot voice that said, "Hello, this is the private number to M-dot-A-dot-X-dot-X-dot. If you wish to see a child, the age of ten and under, dial 1; if you wish to submit a child aged five and under, dial 2; if you wish to join our operation, dial 3, Mar-ie Eli-zabeth Winter-field."

By this time, Marie's eyes were as wide as saucers. She ripped the phone away from her ear and slammed it down.

She looked at Ann, "The other Maxx!"

Ann gasped, "Oh, that might take me a little longer. Give me about two to three hours."

Marie sighed, still shaken, and said, "Sure."

Ann ran out.

Maxx sat in the café and waited.

He got a message from Ann to meet them at the café.

He rolled his eyes, *Typical, I'm right on time, and they're late.*

He sat there and looked around. The walls of the Beaverdale Café were painted baby blue, and the trim was salmon pink. There were quite a few people there considering that it was a small café. Every eye seemed to veer in Maxx's direction at one point or another.

"I hate this place," he said to himself.

Right there, he saw Ann come in the door. Just Ann, but it was okay. He trusted her.

She walked over to him and sat down nervously.

He looked at her and noticed that she didn't make eye contact. He sat forward, "What's wrong?"

She glanced at him and chuckled nervously, "Oh, well. It's nothing. I just heard that you're not supposed to stare at the eyes of the patient of M.A.X.X. No offense."

He sat back and chuckled, "Well, technically, you're not supposed to stare at anyone. It's rude. But it's okay. I'm not part of M.A.X.X. anymore, so you can look all you want."

He gave her a cocky smile.

She rolled her eyes, "Lucky me."

He asked, "How old are you anyway? You seem way too young to be working in the SNOW building. Not that I don't seem young for what I'm doing."

Ann looked down and mumbled, "I just turned seventeen. I just got the promotion from Marie." Her voice cracked when she said, "Everyone always joked about my age before the promotion. I wasn't even that high ranking."

Maxx could tell that this was starting to get emotional.

She said solemnly, "Even my parents said that I would never make it in an industry like this one. I always dreamed big, but they always said I could dream, but they would never come true."

Maxx tried to cheer her up, "Well, here you are. They were wrong. You're the second most important person in the industry."

This only made things worse.

She said, "Yes, and I wish they could see me." Suddenly, she started crying.

At this, Maxx was startled. He had no clue how to stop someone from crying.

He scooched over to her and hesitantly put his arm around her shoulder, "Don't cry. What's the matter? I'm sure that they would be very proud of you."

This made things even worse.

Her sobs turned into bawling. She could not stop the tears. She managed, "No, they wouldn't!" She was crying so hard that people started looking.

Maxx was getting very nervous. The eyes were watching him.

Some big biker-sized guy with a full beard said, "Are you bothering this young lady?"

He let go of Ann and said, "No way. I'm not like that."

Some nosy old lady who was listening in said, "I heard him say that her parents wouldn't approve of her!"

The whole café gasped.

Maxx was getting very, very uncomfortable, "What? No, I didn't. That lady just lied."

The old lady growls, "Is that young lady pregnant, and you wouldn't make her honest?"

Ann gasped, "What?"

Maxx had no idea how this happened, but the chair that Ann was sitting on broke, and she fell on the ground. Maxx's eyes were as wide as saucers when someone in the crowd yelled, "He just pushed her off the chair!"

Maxx said quickly, "No, she's fine. See?"

He yanked her up to her feet.

The big fat biker man pointed at Maxx, "That poor girl is all disoriented!"

Maxx chuckled nervously, "Look everyone, it's fine. I'm twenty, so it's all good." He leaned back, proud of his age.

Then some super over-pregnant lady yelled, "Is that supposed to make us feel better?"

Maxx looked at the pregnant lady who was surrounded by little boys.

The old lady snapped and growled, "We don't like your kind here."

Maxx got up and said urgently, "Good because we were just leaving anyway."

He grabbed Ann's arm and lifted her up to her feet, "What about Marie?" she asked.

Maxx whispered to her fiercely, "You're not making this any easier, Ann."

Some kid in the café yelled, "He just threatened her!"

Maxx's eyes were wide.

The biker man was angry and lunged for Maxx.

Maxx dodged him and ran past him but noticed that he was trapped.

Every living soul in the café started to circle him. Even the fish in the tank seemed to be trying to get out after him.

Over where Ann was sitting, the big biker man walked up to her and grabbed her, lifting her off her feet, "Ann, you know better than to be wandering around with mongrels like him. I know what you're going to say that you're seventeen and you have your own life. But what would mom and dad think of you?"

Ann was confused; she looked at this biker man who had a big bad beer belly, hair longer than Spanish moss, a beard that covered his face, and skull tattoos all over his arms and face, yet he was talking to her like he actually knew her.

She asked, "And who are you?"

The guy's eyebrows narrowed, and he grabbed his beard and pulled it down, "It's me, Marian. Don't tell me you didn't recognize me. I'm your brother for Pete's sake."

Ann was horrified by the look of Marian.

He put his beard back and said, "I don't want you near this man again."

Ann said, "You're not my father. Besides you don't even know who he is."

Marian rolled his eyes, "Sure, I do. Marc, the blind man from the other night. You don't think I can tell that he is your boyfriend!"

Ann gasped, "What? You don't know what you're talking about!"

Marian kept going, "And is it true? Are you pregnant?"

Ann was fed up with this, "Let me go!"

Marian put her down, and she ran the other way.

Over where Maxx was, everyone was surrounding him.

The old lady said, "You better look forward to your seat in jail, punk."

Maxx waited for the perfect moment.

Right when all the people lunged at him, he leaped up and grabbed a ceiling fan, which he used to launch himself on the other side of the café. He grabbed a chair and smashed the window.

Ann ran up to him, "Sorry."

He shook it off and grabbed her arm, "Come on!"

They both jumped through the window and onto the sidewalk.

The old lady inside yelled at them, "He's forcing that poor girl to follow him!"

Maxx didn't stick around to find out what else the old hag would say. Because he knew that where there was attention from civilians, M.A.X.X. wouldn't be far behind.

As if on cue, five black vehicles squealed around the corner.

Ann stood there wide-eyed and stared at the vehicles.

She looked at Maxx or where Maxx used to be.

He was gone!

She looked around franticly, "Maxx! Maxx!"

Suddenly, quicker than ever, someone grabbed her and yanked her down, down to a deep dark, stinky place.

She looked around, but all she saw were the green- and brown-stained walls of what looked like a giant pipe, "Wait, is this the sewer?"

Maxx quietly shushed her, "Shhh! Come on." He headed down the gross path, and Ann reluctantly followed him.

After a couple minutes of trudging down the slimy pipe, Ann whispered, "What about Marie? She'll be waiting for us."

Maxx snapped turning to look at her, "Well, you blew my cover! No one blows my cover!" He continued walking.

She looked down and defended herself softly, "I said I was sorry, Maxx."

Maxx sighed, "It's okay. Let's just get out of here."

Chapter Ten

Saturday, December 4, 11:00

At New York Veterans Cemetery, two blocks away, a woman with green eyes and blond hair stood staring at a headstone that read:

Captain K. Winterfield
Born December 4, 1995—Died November 15, 2047
Colonel of FBI, Father, Friend
We Will Forever Miss You, Captain

Two big tears dripped down Marie's face, "I'm sorry, Dad, and I know it is probably too late to say this, but you were wrong. I can't do this by myself. M.A.X.X. is more than a person. If it was just one person like we thought, then I could handle it, but literally hundreds of thousands of people, maybe more, are active members of M.A.X.X." She wiped her face with her sleeve, "I can't take on that many people by myself. I'm only one person. I won't—I can't do this without you." She stepped forward and set her hand on the stone.

Marie noticed a bum leaning on a nearby tree, the wind must have shifted because now she not only could see him but also could smell him.

Marie was saddened even more when she realized that of all the things that could remind her of her dad, it was the smell of an outhouse that made her think of him.

The smell brought her back to the last time she talked with him, that night that the M.A.X.X. case had started. The pipes were bursting all over town, and she was more discouraged than ever. Her dad told her, "You are capable of more than you think, Marie. More than you think."

"Thanks, Dad, you were right. Besides, I'm not alone. I have Maxx, Ann, and Jason to help me out, and we are a family," she said cheeringly before loading up in her Import car and driving to the café.

Marie walked confidently down the sidewalk toward the café. She stood at the doors with her head held high—until she noticed the chaos.

The window was broken, and the authorities were walking all over the place.

Then, a face stood out among the crowd…a big fat biker man, who was crouching down, hiding obviously from her.

Marie instantly recognized this man, "Marian! What are you doing here? And why are you dressed like that?"

Marian froze and then slowly stood up. He looked at Marie, as she walked over to him.

Marie stared, "What are you doing here?"

He said, "Well, Pop told me to investigate undercover what you and Ann were up to. And I saw Ann hear with that 'quote…un-quote' blind street man, Marc. So I turned the whole café against them. They both fled through the window. I knew that Marc was a dirty rat. Next time I see him, he's gonna pay."

"What, so now you're gonna track down Marc, instead of Maxx? Your boss won't be too happy," Marie said quickly.

Marian does a double take and said thoughtfully, "You're right. I guess I'll keep looking for Maxx. It is my job, but I will track Marc on my off time."

He walked away. Marie sighed and shook her head as he walked away, "Where are you guys now?"

She knew from experience that when it came to Maxx, he could be anywhere.

But this time, Ann was with him, and though she was only three years younger, she had no experience, Maxx's chances of being caught just rose considerably with Ann.

"How much longer do we have to be down here? My breaths are getting harder by the minute."

Maxx said nothing to Ann's comment.

Ann looked at him and said, "Sorry about all that commotion up there."

Maxx still said nothing.

Ann ran in front of him, stopped him, and said, "Look, I don't have my notebook. I lost it. So I'm gonna need to talk to someone."

He let out a huge breath as if he had been holding it the whole time and wheezed, "Okay. You're forgiven." Then he walked past her.

She gave a sigh of relief and said to him, "So what's it like? You know, living off your wits and running from the law, trying to avenge all those kids at the organization?"

He let out another huge breath, "I've been meaning to ask you something. How do you know all that stuff? I never told you about it, nor Marie."

Ann said timidly, "Well, I overhear things. I knew about your and Marie's first meeting place at Applebee's. That she hated those cheesy broccolis. I know how you escaped there, and I also know that it was the same way you escaped M.A.X.X."

Suddenly, Maxx grabbed her arm and pulled her into a darker side tunnel as if the underground sewage wasn't enough coverage.

It all happened so fast for Ann. Right there in the small tunnel, she sat on something that she didn't want to think about five inches in front of Maxx's face.

Maxx said quietly and softly, "How do you know that? You weren't even there. No one was."

Ann said quietly trying not to breathe in, which surprisingly smelled like gum, "I heard Colonel Pop talking about your great escape a few years back."
Maxx looked puzzled, "How the heck would Colonel Pop know…" his voice trailed off and his face flooded with realization, "Colonel Pop. Pop! As in P.O.P. He is the guy I've been looking for! Colonel Pop is Percy Owens Peterson." He turned his attention back to Ann, "Thank you. You just gave me everything I need."

Ann grimaced, "Glad I could help. Now can we resume our personal boundaries, please?"

Maxx scoots closer to her and said seriously, "Hey, I'm sorry about your parents."

She suddenly got sad and mumbled, "I said personal boundaries, but whatever…"

He asked, "How'd it happen?"

She gasped, "Oh, they're still alive. Just on vacation."

Maxx raised his eyebrows, "Oh. Okay." He laughed a bit, "Well, the way you were crying back there made me think that something happened."

She laughed too, then got serious, "No. They just left me with Marian. My unstable big brother. Sometimes, he threatens me, and I get scared."

Maxx asked, "Threatens you how."

She shrugged, "Nothing too serious, just my life."

She chuckled, but Maxx saw nothing funny about it. He knew that Marian was straight from M.A.X.X. and was still in it and indeed wouldn't hesitate to kill her on the spot if he had to. And Maxx couldn't let that happen. He's seen many deaths in his life, and he didn't want this innocent girl to be another one of them not just because she was an innocent girl.

She tried to lighten the mood, "Well, where to now?"

Ann was relieved when Maxx stood up and said, "If Marie had something important to tell us, then we need to find out how to contact her."

Ann stood too making sure to maintain boundaries, keeping to the other side of the pipe, "Also, that big biker man from the café, that was Marian. He's watching us."

Maxx asked, "Did he recognize me?"

Ann shook her head, "He thinks you're that blind man, Marc. He thinks you're my…you know what never mind."

"What? What does he think I am?" Maxx said intrigued.

"He—he—he thought that your hair was awesome; by the way, did you do something new with it? I love it!"

Maxx said whipping it out of his face coolly, "Thanks. Let's go."

They continued down the tunnel. Maxx was smiling super big. He now knew exactly who and where his target was. His search was over. Now it was time for action.

Chapter Eleven

Sunday, December 5, 3:15

Marie slowly walked to her office.

Things just didn't make sense to her. She couldn't piece it together.

When she got to her door, she was in for a surprise.

Inside her office were Colonel Pop and some of his men, and they were tearing up her office.

Men slung her computers on the ground, and others ripped up papers.

She gasped and ran to Colonel Pop, "What are you doing? Stop that! I could press charges! Get out of my office!"

Pop said, "It's not 'your' office anymore. The FBI has taken over your agency. I now have the power to get rid of you."

Marie was horrified, "What? You can't do that!"

Pop shook his head, "We can do anything."

Marie asked fiercely, "Why are you doing this?"

Pop immediately ran up to her and growled in her face, "Because you know something. You know about Maxx and where he is."

Marie said exasperated, "What is it with you and this Maxx guy? Why do you hate him so much?"

Pop had a far-off look and said, "Because he did something that I need to fix."

Marie said, "You can't take this agency. It's my father's agency!"

Pop looked at her, "Not anymore."

Marie held back tears, but Pop had her thrown out of the building.

She headed out to her car, as tears started to stream down her face. She felt horrible, but the truth was that these days, the FBI was the top banana.

Everything her father ever worked for was now gone in the hands of that FBI maniac.

Then something dawned on her. Pop was obsessed with Maxx. Why? This all started with the technology wipeout, but now it was much deeper than that.

Pop stood for P.O.P. She knew that, but why the secrecy?

She drove over to the café; police tape was strewn everywhere. She saw a book in the corner of the table.

"How the heck did CSU miss that?" she asked herself, but she didn't dwell on it. She made sure no one was watching when she ran over there.

It was Ann's notebook. She hid it in her jacket and walked casually to her vehicle.

Sitting inside, she opened Ann's notebook and read as fast as she could.

The news inside the book astonished her. Ann held all the secrets. How did she know these things? All along, she knew why everything was happening like it was. Marie breathed as she took in all this knowledge.

A plan began to form in her head. She knew what had to be done.

She took out a metal bowl (an ashtray), set it outside the vehicle, and put the notebook in it.

Then she took out a match and lit the whole book on fire.

Ashes, now the book was no longer a threat.

Now only she and Ann knew these secrets. 'All of them'. Marie didn't even know if Maxx knew about what she and Ann now knew about.

She picked up the ash bowl and scattered the ashes to the wind.

Then she drove away, ready to take action on her plan.

Ann was sitting in her chair reading when Marian walked in. He seemed concerned but to business, "Ann, I wanted to talk with you about this whole Marc business."

Ann looked up with narrowed eyebrows, "What about him?"

Marian said, "Do you need a cup of water? I'll go get you a cup of water."

Ann put the book down as Marian ran to the kitchen.

He had been fetching her water all morning, along with slippers and breakfast. He even said she could have a dog.

He gave her a cup of water and said, "Listen, I wanted to ask you some questions about him."

Ann scoffed and started to get up, but Marian grabbed her gently and insisted that she sit down, "Why is he always with you and Marie?"

Ann was sort of stumped on what to say when her phone rang.

She reached into her pocket and pulled it out. It was Marie, "Hello?"

Marie said on the other line, "Hi, Ann. I want you to meet me at Applebee's, pronto."

Ann agreed and put the phone in her pocket, "I need to go."

She got up and walked toward the door.

Marian hopped in the driver's seat of the car and said, "I'll drive you."

Ann shook her head franticly, "No, I can drive myself."

Marian was insistent, "I wasn't asking. You're in no condition to drive. You don't want to upset the bunny."

Ann had no idea what he meant by that, but she wasn't sure she wanted to. She sat in the rider's seat and hoped that Marie wasn't bringing Maxx too.

Chapter Twelve

December 2047, sometime in the morning

Applebee's was serving a new special that day, raspberry jellied green beans, with nacho chili sauce on the side, coated in baked bean powder.

Marie was disgusted at the sound of it, but she almost gagged when Maxx crunched down a whole raspberry-green bean and said, "Wow, who knew Applebee's could make such good stuff?"

Marie said, refusing to look at him, "Not me."

A couple minutes later, Ann walked in, and Marian right behind her.

Marie almost screamed at the sight of Marian.

Maxx on the other hand seemed completely composed and self-confident.

Marian and Ann walked up to the table, and Marian said, "Hello, Marie." He gave Maxx the evil eye, "Marc."

Marin sat on the opposite side of the table from where Maxx was sitting.

As Marie thought in her head that she might still be able to pull off her plan, Jason walked in the door, ran to their table, and sat down, "Hi guys. I felt hungry, too."

Ann sat next to Maxx and took a green bean from his plate, giggling, "Wow, these are really good."

Marian and Maxx are giving each other the stair as if everything and everyone was blocked out.

Marie said angrily, "I'm going to get a drink." She got up and walked away.

Jason followed her, "Feeling kind of thirsty myself."

Ann suddenly felt like she didn't belong.

She looked at Marian and Maxx then said, "I've got to go to the…yeah I got to go." She got up and walked away.

Maxx took a drink of his tea.

Marian said, "You look like you're going to pass out. Have you eaten anything today?" He slid a plate of food toward him.

Maxx just looked down.

Marian said, "Let's talk about Ann."

Maxx continued to look down.

Marian scooted forward, "Hey, this means everything to me."

Maxx took another drink of tea and then said, "Are you serious?"

Marian jumped forward, "I knew that accent was fake." Then he sat back again, "Yeah, my mother started from the ground up, with a million-dollar loan from my grandfather; my father owns none of it; and she made him sign a prenup. He lives in fear. And I know I shouldn't say this out loud, but when he told me that I was disowned from the inheritance, I could have killed him, and I did."

Maxx looked at him with a disgusted and disinterested look.

Marian said, "And I don't think it—think it, I know it—know it."

Maxx was confused and didn't know why Marian was telling him this, but all he said was, "If you only knew how suffocating you are."

Marian looked at him and sighed, "Yeah, I know, Pop tells me almost constantly."

Maxx said as he moved his cup of tea away from him, "Why do you care what they think?" then Maxx stood up, "Do you understand that just associating with you could cost me my own inheritance that I'm trapped in." He was referring to M.A.X.X., but, of course, there was no way for Marian to know that.

Marian slowly stood up too.

Maxx turned to Marian and scoffs, "You're not gonna see a penny of profit with the job you are doing." Maxx looked at him and said his name, "Mary Ann."

Marian sort of chuckled and said to him, "I'm going to say this to you, no cameras, no nosey little sisters, just you because you know it's true. Shut up, Marc. Shut up! With that stupid Hitler—German drawl! Is my name Marian? Yes, it is. Am I proud of it? No, I'm not! But that doesn't give you a reason to make fun of it! It's Marian!"

Maxx just stared into the distance for a second.

Then smirked and turned around, "That's what I said. Mary Ann."

Marian's face started to turn red when suddenly all the lights turned off in the whole restaurant.

Maxx was on the floor and ready for action within a second.

The room was pitch-black when suddenly a blue searchlight shined from the door.

Maxx looked around and saw that everyone in the restaurant had guns and was pointing them at him.

Maxx spun around franticly like an animal in a cage, looking for a place to escape. Marian was confused and spooked also.

He saw Marie and Jason in the corner, tied up and chained together.

Suddenly, a figure stepped in the doorway.

Colonel Pop chuckled his evil laugh, "Well, well. I've caught you now, Maxx."

Marian was confused and said, "What? I think you're confused, Pop. This is Marc, my sister's boyfriend that I told you about."

Maxx was caught off guard by Marian's statement, but he was too focused on Pop to say anything.

In the bathroom, Ann poked her head out and gasped.

She slammed the door and ran to the toilet where she struggled to push the toilet.

"He makes this look so easy," she said before the toilet gave way and water spouted out everywhere, "How come that never happens when Maxx does it?" She took out a clip from her pocket and pinched her nose. "Here goes nothing." Then she jumped down to escape.

Back in the main room, Pop snapped at Marian, "Are you blind, Marian? This is obviously Maxx. We have the same nose."

Marian was extra confused, "He had your nose? What?"

Pop literally slapped Marian across his face, "Don't be an idiot!"

Marian regained his composure and said to Maxx, "Maxx? Maxx! You son of a gun. You had me fooled. Who would have thought my sister's boyfriend would such a…wait, Maxx!"

He pulled his gun out and aimed it at him like everyone else finally realizing the predicament.

Colonel Pop turned his attention to Maxx, "Maxx, I am going to enjoy making you regret what you did to—well—M.A.X.X."

Pop nodded to one of his men, and suddenly, someone walked up behind Maxx and slammed him hard in the head. Maxx yelled, stumbled a bit holding his head, and collapsed and passed out.

Chapter Thirteen

Monday, December 6, 2:00 a.m.

Marie woke up with a headache. She took heed of her surroundings. There, she sat on a metal bench inside of a cell with one light in the middle. She heard a groan next to her, and she jumped and saw Jason coming too.

The first thing he said was, "Where's Marc?"

Marie looked around, "I don't know."

Jason got up and said darkly, "They probably have him in a deep dark facility with multiple security systems and guards at every corner."

Marie looked at him and sighed, "You're probably right."

On the other side of the building, in a pitch black, guarded, and secured room, Maxx slowly opened his eyes.

He groaned and started to move his hand to his head, but then he woke up completely and took note of his situation.

His arms were chained not only together but across his chest in an X form. His legs and abdomen were completely locked down with some kind of metal piece that made it impossible for him to move his legs.

There was a chain around his neck that was attached to the ceiling, making it almost impossible to move his neck, and he had a muzzle on that cut off his blood circulation. He was chained down with at least thirty chains.

Plus, just to add on, surrounding him were hundreds of tiny lasers, machine guns, bombs, and even a rocket, all for him If he moved, the whole block would blow up.

He muttered, "Oh, man."

The word was only a muffled noise though.

He heard a shaky voice demanding, "Don't talk."

He glanced over and saw a security guard with a machine gun, outside the cell.

Maxx immediately started looking around for a way to escape.

Suddenly, a voice said, "Oh no. You won't get out of this one. If you so much as have high blood pressure, those bombs will go off."

Maxx looked over and saw Pop stepping out of the shadows.

He mumbled disappointedly, "Oh, man, I should have brought my insulin." But it was only muffled noise.

Pop said, "You can never get out, Maxx. Do you want to know why? Because I designed it myself. If you try anything and I mean anything, this whole room will blow. There are multiple guards outside your cell, plus all these guns, and lasers that were put in. But Maxx, if you do get out of this, then I will stop the chase and order the government to give you an honest reward because you would have achieved the impossible. The unheard of, the unbeatable system."

As he talked, Maxx looked at Pop's pocket and saw a little remote-type devise barely sticking out. It had a button that said: M.A.X.X. CONTROL UNIT. That was the key to turning all this stuff off!

Colonel Pop laughed and walked out.

Maxx sighed and looked down. He could see that there was no way to get out without help.

Marie was sitting down, trying to figure out a way to escape. Jason was pacing the jail cell. He finally sat down with a sigh, "I can't think of anything!"

Marie was about to say something encouraging when they heard a sound down the hall.

Someone hit the floor and passed out.

Marie got up and walked over to the bars.

The guard was on the floor, passed out.

She gasped when suddenly. Ann jumped out of the corner.

Marie jumped back, and Jason stood up. "Ann, what are you doing here?"

Ann said as she fumbled with the keys, "I'm going to get you out." She put the key in the lock and unlocked the door. Jason ran out and hugged her.

Marie was all busyness, "We have to get to Maxx."

Ann wrenched Jason off of her and said, "They have to be holding him in the deepest part of the facility."

She took a map that she had stolen earlier, which showed all the holding spots.

Marie said, "We'll need a distraction."

Ann said smiling, "You and Jason can get a distraction. Let me handle Maxx. And make the distraction good." Ann ran off.

Marie looked at Jason, and he nodded. They headed toward the exit to find a distraction.

Ann headed down a pathway where a guard was posted at the door.

She ran up to him, "Excuse me, sir, I am so lost. Where's the exit?"

She remembered on the map that the deepest lock-up was next to an exit door, which was a bad design.

The guard seemed confused at her presence at first, but then his face relaxed into a smile and he said, "The closest exit is straight down this hall to the right. But don't go left because there's a dangerous criminal called Maxx down there."

Ann nodded and started down the hall.

The guard reminds her, "Remember, right exit, left Maxx."

Ann nodded, "Got it, thanks."

She walked to the end of the hall and peeked back at the guard who wasn't looking at her. Then she slipped left, down the hall.

She went to each door and looked through a fogged-up window.

Finally, she got to one door and saw Maxx all chained up.

She tried to open the door, but it wouldn't budge. It needed a key, and she knew exactly who she could get it from, Colonel Pop.

Chapter Fourteen

A few moments later

Marie and Jason were right outside the building standing in ankle-deep snow.

"What should we do?" Jason asked.

Jason was shivering in the wind; it was already December, and the air was well below freezing.

Marie sighed, "We need something that will force everyone's attention to us."

Jason smiled, "Like an animal. We should go to that pet store over there and take all their dogs!"

Marie looked at the pet store across the street. A couple of small cars were parked in the parking lot. But there were also three huge horse trailers able of fitting at least ten horses. Marie looked at them and was wondering at first what they were doing at the pet store.

She smiled, "I have a better idea."

She and Jason cross over to the other end of the street and up to the man in the first truck.

He looked out the window at her and blew a puff of smoke.

"Excuse me, sir, but how many horses do you have in these trailers?" Marie asked politely.

The man scoffed and blew her off, "What are you, the horse police? Ha."

Marie looked at Jason, then back at the man. She flashed her badge at him and stepped closer, "Let's try this again."

The man looked worried.

Ann saw Marian standing next to Pop. She ran up to him, "Marian."

Marian looked at her with wide eyes, "What are you doing here? It's not safe."

A deep voice yelled, "Miriam!" Colonel Pop walked over to them.

Marian put his head down, *They can never get my name right.* Marian said, "Sir, this is my sister that I told you about."

Pop looked at her judgingly, "The one who was friends with Marc."

Ann smiled casually. She was getting uncomfortable.

Suddenly, the ground literally started shaking. The light flickered, and they could hear a distant rumble getting closer.

Pop, Marian, and Ann ran over to a balcony and saw the most bizarre sight ever.

The big exit door was pounded in with such a force that it fell off its hinges, and in came a huge, angry, fiery red stallion followed by a huge herd of at least fifty horses.

On one of the horses was Marie, and she shouted, "Yeehaw!"

Pop gasped, "What is this?"

Ann said really quickly, "This is my cue."

She grabbed the remote control from his pocket, like a professional thief, and hightailed it out of the room.

Pop gasped and freaked out, "She's got my control!"

Marian and Pop ran to the door.

Suddenly, Marian stopped. His eyes were narrowed and a little scared.

Pop said with his hand on the door, "Come on, Marian. What are you waiting for?"

He opened the door, and Marian's eyes got wide, "Uh, sir?"

Pop sighed and pulled out a gun, "Marian, if you don't come, you're fired."

Pop turned around and was half an inch away from the same enormous red, angry stallion.

The horse neighed super loud and reared up, pawing ferociously in the air.

The scream that emanated from Pop was inhuman.

He slammed the door closed, and it was immediately broken down by the huge body and muscles of the stallion.

Pop screamed again and ran after Marian.

The stallion was mad, and he was indeed a worthy opponent, even to a gun.

The horse stared at Pop as if daring him to use the gun because it would take more than one bullet to take him.

Marian had his eyes wide, "We might have a problem."

Down in the big section of the building, the herd of horses pounded through anything in their way. Desks were toppling over, and the ground seemed to be ready to fall through.

Marie was on top of a pure white horse with Jason behind her.

She kept trying to rile up all the horses and keep things interesting.

All the security guards and FBI men were hiding under desks and behind couches, trying not to get trampled by the big animals.

Maxx was in the cell wondering what the heck was going on out there.

The ground was shaking, and he could hear a bunch of noise.

Suddenly, his cell door was pounded in.

He jumped but couldn't really move anywhere.

It was as if someone got a battering ram to break the door down.

He watched as the rhythmic banging continued.

If he didn't know better, the dents in the door started to look like horse hoof marks.

Suddenly, he heard a loud neigh, and the door was kicked down with an incredible amount of force.

In came a huge red stallion looking at him.

It was totally unexpected. Maxx just stared, and the stallion just stared.

Suddenly, Ann ran out from behind the horse with the key in her hand. Maxx's eyes widen.

He tried to say something, but the muzzle prevented him.

Ann ran over there with the remote key, "Okay, um what button unlocks this thing."

She fumbled with it a little. She pressed a small blue button.

Suddenly, the ceiling opened up, and out came a huge machine gun down to his head aimed and ready.

Maxx gasped and squeezed his eyes shut. Sweat trickled down his forehead.

Ann grimaces and looked at the remote, clueless.

Maxx watched in disappointment.

Ann could not go near Maxx because there are lasers everywhere. Ann breathed, "Here goes nothing."

She pressed the big red button.

Suddenly, all the lasers disappeared, and all Maxx's restraints loosened.

Maxx jumped up and ripped the muzzle off his face.

He ran toward Ann and said, "You're a crazy girl for coming after me you know, that right?" Then he kissed her forehead.

Ann smiled a bit and blushed.

Maxx took the remote and put it in his pocket, straight back to business, "Go get Marie and Jason and get out of here. I'll take it from here."

Ann nodded and ran out the door.

Maxx took out the remote and smiled. He had an idea.

Then he heard a snort behind him.

The big red stallion hadn't followed Ann but was still with him, just standing there. His ears were tilted backward, and he seemed angry.

Maxx looked at the horse and smiled. He had a better plan just then.

Marie knocked over a desk, reviling two men hiding from the rage of the horses.

She laughed comedically and said, "Surrender or die!"

The building was still filled with horses, and they were still wild because Jason was screaming and railing them up.

Ann ran into the confusion and spotted Marie.

She ran to Marie who was chasing guards away as she rode a white horse.

Ann athletically leaps onto the back of Marie's horse, like a professional vaulter. She said to Marie, "We have to go!"

Marie screamed when she realized that Ann was right behind her.

The white Arabian mare's ears went back, and she was spooked by the scream, along with all the chaos.

Marie looked back at Ann with wide eyes and said, "Where's Maxx?"

Ann said blushing again, "He said that he would take it from here and that we need to get out."

Marie nodded and turned her pure white Arabian horse around and went toward Jason.

The building was filled so tightly with horses, and they were constantly bumping into them.

Ann backflipped off of Marie's horse and straight onto another. This one was a uniquely designed piebald paint horse.

Ann followed Marie.

Marie was heading straight for Jason, who was chasing around some colts, unintentionally dodging kicks left and right.

She reached out her arm and snatched him right up and onto the back of her horse.

They gallop their horses out the busted-down door, and many of the other horses ran out as well.

Colonel Pop and Marian ran over to Maxx's cell.

"This better not be Maxx's doing," Marian muttered.

They both stopped cold when they reached Maxx's cell.

There on the floor was the battered and misshaped door to his cell.

Pop was furious, and he walked into the cell saying, "Impossible!"

He walked through the door and was stopped short when he sees on a table; there was a sign that said, *Run.*

Marian gasped behind him, and he saw a cheery bomb, with the fuse burning low.

It jolted them into action. Pop yelled and ran out.

Marian hot on his tail; Pop jumped on the floor and yelled to everyone in earshot, "Take cover!"

He covered his head and waited in agony.

Nothing.

Nothing.

He lifted his head and thought about it. Anger was starting to boil inside of him.

He yelled in outrage, "Maxx!"

Outside, in the snow, only one block from the building, stood Ann, Marie, and Jason.

They waited at a makeshift table in the back of Applebee's, while a few horses still ran around outside.

Down the road came Maxx galloping on that big red horse.

A few pedestrians scattered away from this giant horse coming by.

Maxx spotted them and stopped the red horse close by.

He hopped off the big horse and jogged over to them, "Everyone okay?" he immediately noticed the unease of the group.

They all nodded.

Maxx could tell that the mood was tense.

Suddenly, Marie stood up, her back facing Maxx, and she said, facing Ann, "How could you do that!"

Ann was shocked, "What?"

Marie said, "You just come in with Marian right behind you! Do you have any idea how much time and work I put into not being caught?"

Ann said something that Maxx knew wasn't normally like her, "You don't like the fact that I won."

Marie said angrily, "No, this is when you be quiet and listen! I did not do all this work, just to have it screwed up by you! You may be happy with this, but I am not! I am done here."

Marie turned around and started to walk away when Maxx ran up to her, "Hey, what do you mean by you're done here? You can't quit."

Marie said with determination, "Working with you sounded good at first, but people change."

Maxx said quickly and pleadingly, "Hey, I'm still me."

Marie looked at him, "Not you, me."

Maxx took a breath and flashed his smile, "Oh good, that would make more sense because I am exactly the same."

Marie said, "I meant what I said that I want to remember this case, but it's getting too out of hand, Maxx."

She turned around and got on her Arabian, and she rode away.

Maxx was hurt, as he watched her ride away, "Did she really just leave?"

Jason whispered in the back, "Yeah."

As if things weren't bad enough, they heard the engine revving.

Maxx, Ann, and Jason looked at the noise, and out of the fog came many, many black cars.

Maxx's eyes widened, and he yelled, "We got to run!"

He grabbed Jason and jumped onto the red stallion. Ann was not far behind on her paint horse.

They started galloping down the road.

The chase was on. Chase three…

Regardless of the fact that the big red horse was really fast; the ones chasing them still had cars, M.A.X.X. Cars no less, and they sped up to them fast.

Maxx knew that he stood no chance, and he noticed Ann, struggling a bit on her paint horse.

He reached back with his arm, grabbed Jason, and threw him onto Ann's horse, while they were in mid-gallop.

Jason screamed, arms flailing, but landed perfectly behind Ann.

Maxx yelled, "They're after me. You two get out of here."

Jason yelled franticly, "No, what about you!"

Maxx said, "I can handle it, just go!"

Ann hesitated but knew that it was necessary and turned her horse, and they disappeared into the snow.

Maxx smiled sadly, then got to business, "Alright, Xavier. Let's see how fast you can really run." (He was talking to his horse.)

The big stallion pinned his ears back and surged forward at a faster pace, kicking up snow until he reached the plowed road.

Maxx turned him down to an ally where only his horse could fit. The triumph wasn't long though; as soon as he went out the other side, black cars surrounded and sped at him.

Maxx galloped in the opposite direction. They were heading downtown, and the stallion snorted in irritation as the cars kept swerving around him.

Riley Xavier Xanthus (the horse) was a good sport through it all, but the black cars got the better of it.

One vehicle stopped in front of him suddenly, and it made Xavier freak and slip, throwing his rider, Maxx, straight onto the windshield of the black car.

Maxx held back a yell when the impact came, and he tried to push down the knife-like pain that shot through his arm and leg.

Things were happening so fast. He jumped up and ran over behind a building, barely dodging the men after him.

The black vehicles started to follow him but could not fit into the narrow alley.

Many men in SWAT suits jumped out and went after him. They had their guns loaded and on their side.

Maxx paid no attention to the fact that he was limping down the street, but many civilians noticed and starred.

A small apartment was the closest building for cover. There was a small luminous sign that said, 'Nikki Shorts Apartments For Losers With No Money'.

He ran in and slammed into the front desk, spooking the desk woman.

"I need to get to the roof!" he demanded.

The woman took in the sight of him and stammered a bit.

Maxx yelled again and slammed the desk with his fist, "The roof!"

The woman said quickly and pulled out a card, "Okay, here."

Maxx snatched it from her hand and ran over to the stairs. He learned never to trust elevators.

The woman at the desk was already spooked when Colonel Pop, Marian, and thirty SWAT men came running in.

Pop demanded of the woman at the desk, "Where did he go?"

The woman took in the sight of this whole scene, and she stammered a bit.

Pop whipped out a gun and pointed it right at her forehead, "Where did he go?"

She stammered more, terrified. A lady behind her quickly said, "He went to the roof."

Pop immediately ran to the elevator, followed by Marian and all the SWAT men.

They got to the roof, but no one was there. It was a small, flat roof. A couple of potted plants sat at the edge. There was also a satellite dish, but no Maxx.

Pop narrowed his eyebrows and looked around. He had to be here somewhere.

Pop said, "Maxx, I know you're up here."

Suddenly, Maxx's voice came from behind him, "Your right."

Immediately, everyone swiveled around and pointed their guns toward Maxx, but they were surprised at what they saw.

Pop hadn't pulled his gun out because it wasn't there. In front of him stood Maxx holding him at gunpoint with Pop's gun.

Maxx warned the other people, "If any of you shoot, I'm going to kill him, your leader. Don't think I won't."

This stopped all the other men from shooting on sight. They all knew that people who had had the M.A.X.X. formula will do anything to stay alive. Anything.

Pop soothed it over with a comment, "Well, I got to hand it to you, snatching my gun was quite clever."

Maxx made a disgusted look and said, "Yeah. I know. I am like that sometimes."

Pop unexpectedly smiled really big and said, "Yes. I was so proud of you. You were going to be the new face of M.A.X.X." Then his face grew dark, "Then you had to go and run away, making yourself a fugitive."

Maxx was disgusted, and he scorned, "That's because I saw what it was, what M.A.X.X. really was. You take over the lives of innocent children to make your own personal army! And you manipulated me into it when I was five years old. Five! It was all I knew."

Pop tried to soothe, "I give children more ability than they could dream of. I give them hope for the future."

Maxx's grip on the gun, and mostly, the trigger, tightened. He scoffed, "Hope for the future. You don't care about them. You never cared about anyone but yourself."

Pop shook his head and took a step forward, "No. I cared about you. How could I not? You are amazing Maxx, and you could have gotten better."

Maxx shook his head in disgust, "You just wanted power."

Pop said gently, "No, I wanted you, Maxx."

Maxx made a confused and weirded-out face.

Pop smiled and said, "Haven't you ever wondered why you're so talented? You're my son."

Maxx's mouth literally dropped, and he was on the brink of blowing this man away, but something stopped him. If his grip could get tighter, it did.

"How dare you, insult me in such a...weird way like that?" He said.

Pop grinned and said, "You are my son, Maxx. You remember, remember way back, those times I would visit the house. All those things I gave you on your birthday. I even made you the best operative that M.A.X.X. ever had. You were so close to perfection; you could have been me."

Something in Maxx's head told him, *Enough chit-chat.*

Maxx lifted the gun, aimed, and fired. The shot wasn't just from his gun.

Marian had taken a shot, and so did Maxx at the same time.

Marian's bullet hit Maxx's gut, and the other one got Pop's shoulder.

The gunshot would have hit a bull's-eye to the chest if Maxx hadn't stepped over an empty pot and tripped. He fell down and found himself hanging off the side of the building by one arm.

If Maxx hadn't been shot, he would have been able to pull himself up no biggy.

He glanced at his wound and could tell it was bad. He felt strength draining out of him, and one hand slipped off the edge of the roof that was holding him.

Marian's face came into view, and he was reaching out to Maxx.

"Take my hand!" he was saying.

"No! Do you actually think I would trust you? I might as well jump now!" Maxx let go and fell down, down into the dark, thick fog.

Pop stood and watched it all. His outrage and pain were clear; he was angry. He turned around to Marian and yelled, "Did I tell you to shoot? No! I should have fired you long ago, Marian! Get out of my sight!"

Marian put his gun back and his head down and walked back to the stairs.

Pop leaned over the edge of the building and looked into the fog.

"There's no way anyone, even from M.A.X.X., could survive a fall like that." Pop turned around and walked back to the elevator. All the other men followed.

Down the road, the big red stallion Riley Xavier Xanthus galloped full speed down the road careful to doge the ice spots. He was spooked and mad. His ears were pinned back, and his head was down. As he ran, he scattered countless pedestrians. He was tracking the scent of his fellow horses, Ann's and Marie's horses, and he found them at a small, half hidden, house, tied up. It was Maxx and Jason's house. The place was covered in vines, and it looked as though no one would dare live there.

Ann, Jason, and Marie were outside, next to the horses.

Marie and Ann gasped as the stallion approached spooked and upset.

Jason whispered in horror, "Where's Maxx?"

Ann's eyes were wide, and her brown skin was pale.

Marie breathed, "Oh no!"

Ann tried to shrug this off, but her voice was shaky, "He's fine, I'm sure. He…he probably just got off the horse

to, I don't know, put his pursuers down the wrong path…"
She was starting to get panicky, "He's survived worse thing
than this, right? He's fine, guys. He'll show up soon, come
on."

Marie stopped her, "Ann, maybe your right." She
glanced at Jason, obviously trying not to scare him, "I'm
sure he'll show up. Let's get inside." Marie walked Jason
inside.

Ann followed. She didn't like to admit it, but she was
genuinely freaked out right now. She could not accept that
Maxx might not come back.

Chapter Fifteen

A few milliseconds after Maxx's fall

Felicity Obrien, a ninety-year-old woman with dementia, was outside 'Nikki Shorts Apartments For Losers With No Money', at the side of the pool 'sunbathing'…at 11:00 at night…in the snow.

She had her sunglasses on, and she was happy that she was finally getting that tan that she had been working on for years.

As she laid, there on her reclining chair, something fell in the pool. Something so big that it sent a huge wave of icy water onto her.

She gasped and took her sunglasses off to see what it was.

"Edward!" she called, "There's a dog in the pool!"

An even older man fumbles out of the hotel building, "Felicity, what are you doing out here? You could catch your death of cold."

Felicity pointed to the pool.

Edward put his prescription glasses on and looked in the pool, "That's not a dog, Felicity. It's a person. It is a good thing that they didn't drain this pool."

Felicity almost jumped for joy, "Oh, it's Peter!"

Edward shook his head, "Don't be daft, Felicity. Peter's in London." Edward took a closer look at this man, "He's hurt, but he is alive. We need to take him in and bandage up that wound. Let's get him out of the water before it freezes again with him in it. Felicity, find the wheelbarrow."

Felicity jumped up, "Anything for Peter."

This man was completely knocked out cold, so it took all of Edward's and Felicity's strength to get him out of the pool, through the apartments, up the elevator, and to their room.

As they pulled him in the wheelbarrow through the lobby, the desk woman saw them, and her face turned pale.

She recognized this man as the one who ran to the roof.

She stood up and yelled, "That's it, I quit! I didn't get this job so I could be in the middle of a crime scene! I just wanted peace and quiet!" She grabbed her coat and stormed outside.

Maxx's arms and legs were dragging on the floor because the garden wheelbarrow was so small.

Eventually, they got him to their room.

There was a trail of blood left behind, and the pool was red.

"It's okay, Peter. We'll take good care of you. Mummy got you." Felicity said as Edward struggled to get him on their couch.

"Can you help him, Edward?"

Edward took in the look of his patient's wound, "He's been shot in his abdomen. He's lucky, two inches to the right, and it would have gotten his stomach. But it doesn't look like anything major has been damaged."

Felicity got a steaming hot, damp rag, and put it on his head, "It's okay, Peter. Mummy and daddy got you."

Edward said, "I'm going to need to take that bullet out."

Felicity asked, "How do you do that?"

Edward looked at her and said trying to get ready, "It'd be best if you went outside and cleaned up that mess, while I deal with this."

Felicity nodded her head, "Ah, yes, of course."

Then, suddenly, Maxx turned his head and groaned.

Edward said, "He's coming to."

Felicity clapped her hands together, "Oh, Peter, your awake."

Maxx had a look of pain on his face as he moves his hands to his wound.

Edward put his hand on his shoulder, "Stay still."

Maxx looked at him and Felicity, with a perplexed look, "What? Who are you?"

Felicity gasped offended, "I can't believe you don't remember your own parents, Peter."

Maxx wheezes out, "What? Who's Peter?"

Edward told Felicity, "Felicity, clean outside. Remember?"

She gasped, "Oh, yes." She turned and walked out.

Edward said to Maxx, "That bullet needs to come out."

Maxx came to grips with what that meant.

He breathed slowly and said, "Well, let's get it over with."

Edward feebly walked over to his lighted candle.

Maxx watched as he took out a knife and was heating it over the small fire.

Maxx asked him, with a hint of nervousness, "So you've done this before, right?"

Edward smiled, "Yes. I was a doctor back in the eighties. Of course, none of my patients ever survived but spatter spat."

Maxx gasped and fidgeted on the couch.

Edward reassures him, "Don't worry though. I know exactly how to do this."

Maxx was very nervous. His life was in the shaky hands of this old man.

Edward shuffled over to him with his hot knife, "Ready? Now just lay back and bite this."

He gave him a piece of wood to bite. Maxx hesitantly put it in his mouth. Edward leaned down next to the couch and lifted Maxx's shirt, just to reveal the wound.

"Here it went," Edward said.

Maxx squeezed his eyes shut and prepared for the worst.

Edward brought the knife centimeters away from the gunshot wound, "Now what did Dr. Deming say?" He took a breath and went for it.

Out next to the pool, Felicity had a broom and was unsuccessfully trying to sweep up the frozen blood from the tile floor.

Colonel Pop and Marian ran onto the scene and saw Felicity cleaning up the blood.

Pop asked the old woman, "Where did all this blood come from?"

Felicity chuckled and said, "Oh, Peter had a bloody nose again."

Pop and Marian looked perplexed. That was a lot of blood from a bloody nose.

Marian pointed, "Look. The blood comes from the pool. He isn't dead."

Pop sighed, "Yes, but he can't be far. We will search the ground. Put this motel on lockdown. No one comes or goes. Now!"

Marian jumped and ran from the scene.

Maxx groaned painfully, squeezing his eyes closed, as Edward wrapped the wound.

"They're all better." Edward seemed really cheerful, and it aggravated Maxx.

Maxx just put his arm over his eyes to conceal his facial expression and tears.

Suddenly, Felicity ran in, if you can call that slow movement running, and she said, "There are big hooligans outside looking for Peter."

Edward snapped, "What are you blathering about now, Felicity?"

Felicity breathed, "I told them that Peter had a bloody nose, and they locked down the building!"

Maxx sat up slowly and groaned, "They're after me. I got to go."

He started to get up when immediately Edward and Felicity sit him back down, "You need to stay and rest."

Maxx tried to reason, "They are coming for me, and they will kill whoever is in their way."

Felicity looked perplexed, and she asked Edward, "What did he say?"

Edward sighed and said to her and to Maxx, "He was speaking nonsense. He will stay as long as he needs to. Right, Felicity?"

Felicity gasped, "Oh, of course!"

Edward said to Maxx, "Now don't make me have to tie you to the couch. You stay put. We'll deal with those hooligans outside."

Maxx's eyes widened as Edward and Felicity both headed outside the room.

They were actually going to try to get rid of Pop.

And if Pop or Marian saw them resisting, they're gonna check this room first.

Edward and Felicity walk into the hallway, where Pop and Marian were breaking down doors.

Edward wobbled up to Marian and slapped him on the shoulder, demanding, "You men are disrupting the peace. I could call the authorities."

Pop had a cast on his arm, and he walked to Edward and said while showing his badge, "I am the authorities. Check this man's room."

Marian grabbed Edward by the arm and forced him to show his room. They walked down the aisle as Felicity followed, feebly trying to stop them.

Marian and Pop busted the door open. They all came into the room, filling it within a second. Maxx was nowhere to be found.

The room was filled with SWAT people. Their guns were loaded and ready.

Even the blood on the couch was all cleaned up and tidy.

Pop looked around suspiciously, while Marian pushed everything over and ransacked the place.

Edward ran up to Pop, "You get out of my room this instant!"

Marian looked at Pop and shook his head. There was a chorus of, "Clear!" from all the other men in the room.

Pop looked at Edward and smirked a bit, "My apologies." He motioned for everyone to exit the room.

Within the second, the room was empty of SWAT men.

Felicity seethed as she closed the door, "What hooligans? If they didn't have those silly-looking badges, I'd spit on them. Where's Peter?"

They looked around for an hour.

"He is nowhere to be found," said Felicity as she and Edward stopped in the kitchen.

Suddenly, the floorboard started to move.

Felicity looked horrified and whispered to Edward, "Those rats have really outgrown themselves since last year."

The creature under the floorboard lifted up out of the ground. First, they saw hair, then eyes. Then the rest of the head popped out of the ground, Maxx's head.

Felicity laughed a bit, "Oh, Peter. What are doing down there?"

Maxx grunted in pain as he pulled himself out, "Oh, you know, just fixing the pipes."

She laughed as Edward walked over to help him up. Maxx stood up, holding his side, keeping pressure on it.

Edward scorned him, "I told you to rest. If you keep this up, then you're gonna have to stay here longer."

Maxx sighed as he sat on the couch and carefully laid back.

Edward told him, "Now you stay there. It'd be best for you to just sleep." But, by the time Edward finished his sentence, Maxx was surprisingly, already knocked out cold.

Chapter Sixteen

Some time in December 2047

Marie sipped her cup of coffee, as she, Ann, and Jason sat at the table.

Ann was biting her nails, "What are we going to do?"

Marie said carefully, "We need to continue with the plan."

Jason intervened, "I wasn't aware we had a plan."

Marie explained, "When I rode away after we escaped, I investigated a bit. It turned out that M.A.X.X.'s headquarter is at the Pentagon. But this information was top secret." Marie sniffed softly, "My father died protecting these top-secret documents."

Marie pulled out a bundle of paper, "I got these printed out from security cameras in the FBI room that night. Now the camera footage shows here that the kids in the room were being told to do this. I'm sure you're like, 'we already know this'. Well, hear what you don't know, listen to this." She took a recorder out of her bag, "This is an ultra-high-definition sound recorder, aka the UHDSR." She played the track.

The voice they hear is coming straight from the earpiece that the children had, "Do not let him move." At this, the kids held Captain Kernel at gunpoint. "Now check the desk for the files and burn them." At that, the kids had burned the paper. Marie looked away when the man told them to shoot Kernel. That was the end.

Ann looked at Marie, "What's the point of that?" "Did you guys recognize the voice?"

Ann and Jason shook their heads no.

Marie asked them, "By the way, do you think Maxx bought my whole act back there? Me quitting and everything?"

Ann shrugged, "I guess, why?"

Marie said, "Well, listen to this. It's the same night, same time. I put this extractor on the recording; it's like a decoder, and it turned the sound back into the original. This guy's voice was modified to sound different by high, high tech. Now when I put this decoder on, listen to what the voice boiled down to."

Ann and Jason put their heads in closer when Marie pressed play.

When the voice said, "Don't let him move."

Ann and Jason gasped at the voice they hear.

It was the voice of Maxx.

Ann jumped up, "What is this?"

Marie said calmly, "I don't know. That is the voice that it boils down to. But…"

Ann interrupted, clearly upset, "What, now you're saying that Maxx is responsible for your dad's death? Maxx isn't that kind of guy; he would never do that! You don't know him; he is a good person!"

Marie shook her head, "No, all I'm saying is that…"

Ann gasped, horrified, "You're saying that he is still part of M.A.X.X.! What kind of friend are you? You don't believe in him! All he needs is for us to believe in him. He will come through!"

Marie tried to explain calmly, "No, that's not what I'm saying. Listen." Ann and Jason stared at her, "All I'm saying is that either he or these M.A.X.X. people are really good at framing."

Tears prick Ann's eyes, and Jason stood up angry, "My brother is not part of M.A.X.X., or else he wouldn't be trying to stop them…duh. He needs us to save him, not question his loyalty." He turned to Marie with teary eyes and said angrily, "We came to you because we trusted you. Maxx told me not to trust anyone, but I insisted that we couldn't take M.A.X.X. alone. So he chose you, Marie. He chose you when he wouldn't trust anyone else. He knew you were the only one that could help us; he believed in you."

His voice was getting strongly disappointed, "You remember that night when no one chose you for the SNOW program? Even your dad had his doubts, but secretly, Maxx knew, and it's because of him that you even had an agency. No one was supposed to ever know about it. Maxx wants to help people, but he doesn't even care if anybody knew it was him who helped. He is like that. And, despite everything I said to him, he chose you because he saw that you had a good heart. Maybe he was wrong for once." Jason ran out of the room.

Ann sat silently and looked at Marie.

Marie said quietly, "All I was saying is that somehow, they got Maxx's voice in there. I wasn't saying why or how." Marie breathed and said quietly, "We need the information on M.A.X.X. We can put it all in this USB." She pulled out a USB and gave it to Ann.

Ann looked at it, "What the heck is this?"

Marie muttered and rolled her eyes, "Youth. My plan is somewhat bizarre, but it's all I've got. The Pentagon is the headquarters. We need to get inside their computer system, and with this, we need to load everything we can on M.A.X.X. Then it needs to be sent to my former office in the SNOW building. Once it gets there, I'll need to download it, everywhere. And I mean everywhere until everyone in the whole world knows what M.A.X.X. is. It has been hiding in the shadows for far too long; we need to bring it to public."

Ann said, "But, in order to do that, you'll need to get inside your office, and someone else needs to go to the Pentagon. And get inside M.A.X.X.'s headquarters. That is ridiculous and very risky and dangerous."

Marie nodded.

Ann shook her head and sighed, "Oh, what the heck, I'm in."

Jason walked in out of nowhere and put his fist on the table, "I'm in too."

Marie smiled and said, "Listen, Jason, I'm sorry. I didn't mean it like that about Maxx."

Jason laughed a bit and rubbed his red eyes, "It's okay. I'm a big boy."

Marie looked at Ann, and Ann returned the look, "Let's play ball."

Nightfall crept over the subtle apartment.

In room no. 9, Maxx dreamed about M.A.X.X.

He was in a chair and he held a gun in his hand. His commanding officer commanded him, "Kill him."

Maxx sat in the chair, sweating with fear, "What had he done?"

The man yelled and slammed the desk in such a way it made Maxx jump, "You do not ask questions. You carry out orders. This is what you are trained to do."

Maxx looked at the gun in his hand. This was what he was trained to do. Take orders, but from who? What if this was wrong? What if all his life he had been in the wrong?

Some reckless, nut-head kid once told him, "They can't make you do anything, Maxx. You are in control of your own life. You have a choice."

The man said, "This is your only purpose Number One. You were born for this, born into this program. It is all you have. It is all you are."

Maxx got a look of determination. It was all he had. That was enough to depress him the rest of the way. This was all he ever knew. Sweat trickled down his four head. He literally closed his eyes, stood up, and shot the man who was tied up to a post.

The man laughed and stood in front of him, "Maxx, you are the best solder this organization ever had. You will now be the commander over everyone."

Maxx, the name of the whole operation. It was a great 'honor and privilege'.

He was named Maxx because he was strong and followed orders to the T for he was the only fourteen-year-old in the facility who had obeyed all the way to the execution of a man.

Fourteen-year-old Maxx almost smiled at this 'wonderful privilege', but when he looked back at the dead man on the pole, his blood turned cold.

He had seen death before, but when he looked into this man's pale, distant, open eyes, there was a knife-like pain in his heart. One that he had never felt before. He didn't even know this man; perhaps he didn't even deserve to die. Perhaps...it was Maxx who deserved to die instead.

That night, Maxx lay in his bed and cried his heart out, sincerely. He could not stop the tears, and it was as if his eyes opened and saw M.A.X.X. for what it truly was. That night, he made a plan to escape, and he swore on his life that he would do everything in his power to put an end to M.A.X.X. and put an end to the founder of it as well.

Then another image flashed in Maxx's dream, Colonel Pop had his arms open and he said, "Come home, son. He-he."

To these words, Maxx could feel himself coming closer despite his efforts to get away.

"No! No!"

Maxx jumped up from the couch, yelling, "No!"

Immediately, he was reminded of his gunshot wound. He grasped his side and groaned. The dream had come back to his memory. Slowly, he stood up and walked over to the window. He sat on a chair and moved the curtain to look outside.

The stars were shining bright outside, and everything seemed so peaceful and quiet like all was right with the world, but he knew that was far from true.

It was cold in that room, but he was sweating as if it were in the middle of summer.

He had to get out of those old people's houses. Already, he had brought Pop and Marian to their door. The thought of Pop stopped him. The truth was that he was afraid. Afraid that he couldn't stop M.A.X.X. afraid that he couldn't protect the ones he cared about. Afraid he wasn't good enough.

Anyone he came in contact with was in danger. He looked down as the thought pass his mind. He should have never brought Marie into this, or Jason…then he thought with a different emotion or Ann.

The thought of any harm coming to her made his heart twist and knot inside him. Before all that mattered to him was taking down M.A.X.X., he didn't care about anything else, but then he met Ann…

He smiled a bit at the thought of when he first saw her. She pressed the alarm on him. She had that cool, calmness about her that put him at ease, but she was young and inexperienced.

His smile disappeared. He hadn't even known her that long, and he had never felt anything like this before. What M.A.X.X. had drilled into his head was partially true. M.A.X.X. was all he knew.

He was scared what if he was way in over his head? Who was he to think he could put an end to the most powerful organization in the world? He was just one person, and he felt alone in this operation. An alarm jerked him out of his thoughts. It was Edwards's coffee alarm.

Maxx sighed, trying to relax his nerves, "I got to get out of here."

Edward walked out of his room with his robe on. He saw Maxx up and said, "My coffee is ready. Hah."

Maxx faked a smile and looked back out the window.

Suddenly, a knock sounded at the door, and in Maxx's head, everything was silent, all except the continuous knocking.

Maxx looked at the door with caution, as Edward fumbled over to it, "I wonder who that could be?"

Felicity walked out of her room, as Maxx slowly went to a different room and sat down; in case it was someone looking for him.

Edward opened the door and saw a man about six foot four, with super blond hair, with his wife who had red hair, and their four children with blondish-red hair.

Felicity squealed for joy, "Oh, Peter!"

Peter smiled, "Hey, Mom, how are you guys doing?"

They all come into the apartment, and the kids ran into the other room where Maxx was. As Maxx sat on the couch, a little toddler girl walked up to him, "Hello."

He looked down at her and smiled, "Hello."

She smiled and said, "What's your name?"

He smiled and shook her hand, "Maxx."

She said, "Hello, Maxx. Can you read this to me?"

She pulled out a little book.

Maxx chuckled at this adorable little girl when suddenly four more kids stampede into the room and pounce on him yelling, "Yeah, he's going to read a story!"

Maxx yelped as the kids jump on him, accidentally pounding away at his wound.

Peter, his wife, Edward, and Felicity, all come into the room when they hear the ruckus. Peter was horrified when he saw his kids on top of some stranger in his mother and father's room, "Who is that?"

All the kids get off of him as they hear their dad's voice.

Felicity jumped in and said, "Peter, let me introduce you to Peter…wait. Oh, dear."

Peter raised his eyebrows and demanded an explanation.

Maxx raised his eyebrows as in to say he wanted an explanation too.

Edward looked at both of them and explained, "He just needed help, and that's what we are doing, helping him."

Maxx tried to ease the mood by standing up and introducing himself, but that didn't go so well. As soon as he lifted himself from the chair, the pain in his gut increased, and he fell back down in the chair with a yelp.

Peter's wife gasped, "What's wrong with him?"

Edward disregarded her question and asked, "Anyone hungry?"

Peter looked at him and said, "What happened to this man, Dad?"

Maxx corrected him in a hoarse voice, "The name's Maxx."

At that Peter's wife gasped, "You're the one who's all over the news! You're a wanted criminal!"

Peter looked at Maxx and then at his dad, "Dad, you brought a criminal into your home!"

Edward blew this off, "Oh, shuffle puff. Humans are humans, same as you and I."

They walked into the other room.

Peter said to Edward, "Dad, I think you should come to live with me. We have extra rooms, and I don't think it's appropriate for you to be living by yourselves."

In the other room, Maxx sat when the same little blonde girl walked up to him, "Can you read this to me?"

He smiled and leaned in close making a scary face, "But I'm a criminal."

At this, the girl looked into his eyes and smiled. Her hazel green eyes glistened, "So am I." Underneath her arm, she had a red scar in the shape of a number, 650.

Maxx's smile disappeared immediately when he saw it. It was small and barely noticeable, which means that this girl's parents voluntarily admitted her into M.A.X.X.

His heart jumped when he saw that. He looked into this cute little girl's eyes and saw that she believed everything she was taught.

Abruptly, leaving this little girl without an answer, he stood up, ignoring his pain, and walked outside of that room, "I'm going to get some fresh air."

He said to Peter and Edward.

Outside, he walked away—just away. The world was an awful place. Maxx took note of his surroundings as he sat on a bench. People were cruel creatures as well. He took note of the billboard that had 'women's rights' posted all over it. People yelled angrily at each other as they passed the road. They honked their cars aggressively at each other when nobody was violating any traffic laws. The women's rights billboard was advertising that women had a right to their own body in that they could kill their unborn child. Another billboard advertised car racks.

Maxx's senses were keenly picking up all the awful things in the world. He breathed slowly, and his mind rushed through these facts. There were so many terrible companies and terrible people, but the worst of them was in the shadows. It was done in secret so that no one would see them coming. M.A.X.X. was still a huge threat, and one day, it would come out of the shadows just like all these other things had. He had to put an end to it, and he was the only one who could do that. His mind shifted to Marie, Ann, and Jason.

He also had good people to help him. He knew he needed their help because this was too big for any one person. This was too big for him alone. He stood up with a sense of determination and rebirth. The world is a horrible place, but it is the only place they had, so he had to protect it to the best of his abilities. He had to give it his absolute best shot. He needed to get back to Marie, Jason, and Ann.

Chapter Seventeen

They have lost track of time…

Marie's phone rang as she stood at a round table with Ann and Jason.

She answered, "Hello?"

Nobody answered. She looked at the screen, and there was simply a text message that said, *Time Square, 12:01, not early or late.*

She smirked.

Ann asked, "Who is it?"

Marie showed them the text, "It's Maxx."

Ann and Jason gasped, "Well, let's go!"

Marie said, "We better hurry if we are to make it."

It was 11:58.

One minute exactly before the middle of the day, in Time Square, Marie, Ann, and Jason waited.

12:00

Ann was excited and bouncing. In the midst of a hundred people, they see one familiar face, Maxx.

Ann gasped and ran to him.

Marie tried to stop her, "No, it's still 12:00!"

Maxx saw Ann charging for him. He gasped and braced for impact. His first impulse was to run the other way but fought it down. With every muscle in his body tensed, he also covered his wound.

Ann grabbed him with open arms and enfolded him in a huge hug. He was caught off guard by all this emotion, she was crying, "I thought you were gone!"

His eyebrows narrowed, and he put his arms gently around her also, "I'm okay. I'm okay."

Marie and Jason ran over also and hug him too. They were all crying except him and Marie.

Finally, they all get off of him, "What happened?"

He explained, as they walk to the sidewalk, "Pop found me. I got shot and fell into a pool. Then I was being held hostage by an old couple." He said that last part fondly.

Jason laughed, but Marie was all business, "We have a plan."

Maxx said also, "Me too."

Marie told him about their plan. He nodded as she finishes and said, "That could work, I can probably get into M.A.X.X. and get that information." He stopped and put in, "I'll need help though."

Ann jumped on this a little too quickly, "I'll help you." Everyone looked at her, and her cheeks flushed, "I mean, if you need it." Maxx smiled at her.

Jason put in heroically, "I'm also going to help."

Maxx tore his eyes from Ann and looked at Jason, "No way. You're staying home. I'm not going to have my baby brother's stupid head killed because he was involved in a fight that wasn't even his."

Jason's face fell, and he pouted, "What did I do wrong? I never get to do anything!"

Maxx gave his little brother a stern look that meant his mind was made up.

Jason fell silent, and he crossed his arms.

Maxx looked at Marie, "You'll have to get into SNOW, which is under Pop's surveillance."

Marie nodded.

Maxx sighed and said, "Well, in case everything goes terribly wrong, I have a backup plan."

Marie asked, "What is it?"

Maxx raised his eyebrows, "That can probably wait. Let me just say, it is very big…" He paused, "But I think we should try Marie's plan before we do something that dangerous."

Ann and Marie nodded not planning on probing any further. Maxx looked at his team, "It's settled then. Let's get this party started."

He turned his head to Jason and said protectively, "Jason, back to the house."

Jason looked down and said, "Oh, okay."

Finally, the time came. Maxx and Ann looked at Marie.

Maxx confirmed, "You know what to do."

Marie gave him the USB and said, "Yes, don't worry about me, just focus on what you do, and try to hurry also. Both of you have the hardest job. I'll be in my office waiting for the upload."

Maxx nodded and loaded up in one of Marie's white Import cars. Ann got in the rider's side, and Maxx drove away fast and was gone in a puff of snow.

Marie looked at her watch.

It'll take them at least three hours to get all the way to the Pentagon. They would call her when they arrived.

She sighed and quickly walked inside her house to get ready for her part.

Maxx's blood was rushing. This was it; he was going to finally finish his quest. He drove way over the speed limit, to get there faster.

"So, when we get there, we are going to need to go through the sewers again. The same way I got out as you already know, they hate sewers. So do I, but they won't go down there."

Ann asked, "So you know your way around there pretty well?"

He smiled at her, "Believe it or not, I still remember it like the back of my hand."

Maxx's face got sullen at the thought.

She nodded, not noticing, "So all we need to do is get onto their computers and their online system and download all information onto this USB."

Maxx shook his head, "It's not that easy. Their computer systems don't just give away their information. Luckily, they taught me everything about it, so it'll only take me about ten minutes to decode it. Meanwhile, I'll need you to go and hook up the USB to the main controlled computer."

She nodded nervily, "Easy."

He looked at her nervous expression and said, "Hey, it's going to be fine."

She nodded and looked at him. She was nervous, but she had to ask, "Hey, um. When Marie decoded the recording of her dad's office when he died…the voice giving the commands to the kids…who told the kids to kill

Captain…" She swallowed hard, "the voice was yours, Maxx." She looked at him, questioningly.

His face fell slightly, and his eyes started to shift back and forth, but he didn't say anything. Ann could tell it was a sour subject, so she didn't push too hard, but she did keep the pressure. One minute passed, and Ann did not stop her gaze at him.

He cleared his throat and glanced at her, "It was something that we did, back in M.A.X.X." He stopped there.

Ann nodded and decided to push further, "Listen, Maxx. If we are going to work together, we need to learn how to trust each other. Tell me?"

Maxx did not like this conversation, and he pushed away the feeling of jumping out the window.

"Listen, Ann. My days of M.A.X.X. are not pretty. It isn't some fairytale that might make a good story. It was my life; it was all I knew." And he stopped there, continuing his gaze at the road.

Ann probed further, "I know that. But I need to know Maxx. How can you expect me to trust you if you are holding back so much?"

Maxx held back a sigh, "Fine. I was fifteen when it happened. We were doing multiple drills. It was…it was drills of assassinations. We already knew all of this, but we were about to do a job. They recorded all of our voices to catch any faltering and hesitations. Mine was obviously the best, naturally. So they obviously used that recording."

He stopped there and did not meet her gaze. She could not help but laugh.

Maxx narrowed his eyebrows at her sudden happiness. He looked at her as she composed herself, "Sorry. It is nothing…" she said.

Maxx was intrigued now, "What?" for some strange reason, he could not read her expression, and it confused him.

She laughed again but shrugged her shoulders.

Maxx smiled at whatever was so funny, but he was still confused, "I don't get you sometimes."

Ann looked at him and then asked easily, "If you were never influenced by M.A.X.X., what do you think you would be?"

Maxx was caught off guard by the question, but he took careful thought, "Hmm. Honestly, I would probably be a nerd."

Ann raised her eyebrows and laughed, "I don't think so. Maybe more, a cop."

Maxx had to laugh at that one, "I spent my life fleeing cops. I can't imagine myself as one."

Ann suddenly got serious, "In M.A.X.X., did…did anyone get hurt? Did you get hurt?"

Maxx looked serious, "Yes." Ann looked at him, asking for more.

Maxx sighed, "We were always hurt. As kids, when we were first there, we were each, branded with a small number. Except me. I never knew before why they hadn't done it to me in the beginning, but I guess it was because I was the leader's son."

He was looking at the road again, but this time, he added himself in a quiet voice, "And I have hurt a lot of people."

Ann looked at him sadly.

He added, "Innocent people."

Ann felt sorry and she put her hand on his shoulder, "But things are different now, and M.A.X.X. isn't all you have now. You have Jason, Marie, and you have me…we are a family."

At that, Ann could actually feel Maxx tremble a little. His hands shook unsteadily at the wheel and his eyes pricked with tears. He slowly lifted one hand up to his shoulder and he picked up her hand, but instead of throwing it aside, he just lowered it in between them and held it, "Thanks." He said quietly.

Ann smiled widely and burst out with, "I totally love you!"

Suddenly, Maxx's face turned from sad to shocked. He looked at Ann with wide eyes, demanding an explanation.

Ann gasped and quickly fixes it, "I meant to say I totally love this plan because we are so going to win! Yay!"

Maxx put his other hand back on the wheel and tensed up. Ann always had to say something to ruin the mood.

They both just sat tense in their seats.

Now the rest of the trip was going to be long and drawn out.

"Thanks a lot, Ann," Maxx mumbled under his breath.

At her house, Marie had her suit and gun on. She was as ready as ever. It had been two hours, and it was time for her to take action. She loaded up in her car and drove downtown to her former agency. Looking up at the tall building, she waited in her car for Maxx to call.

Maxx sped down the road, only thirty minutes away.

Ann slept soundly, and he was grateful. After her embarrassing outburst, it was as if he was on edge the whole time. He looked at her and was almost frightened to shake her awake. He totally knew how she felt now—about the plan of course, and the scary thing was that he felt the same—about the plan. But only she had a big enough mouth to blurt it out. He reached over and shook her awake, "Hey, we're almost there, better be up and ready."

She rouses awake, "We're there?"

He shook his head, "Almost."

She looked out the window and saw that they are in Maryland heading into Virginia.

She breathed in deeply, "Here we go."

Ann could tell Maxx was getting more and more on edge the closer he got to the Pentagon.

As they drove, she noticed light flurries falling outside.

"Oh, look. It's snowing again."

Maxx nodded, "Yep, it's almost Christmas you've got to expect that kind of thing."

Maxx took out his phone and dialed Marie's number.

At the SNOW building, Marie answered her phone, "Hey, Maxx, you there?"

Maxx answered, "Yup, you?"

Marie said, "Yes. The plan is in action."

Suddenly, Marie heard a grunt in the back of her car.

She gasped and looked back, and to her surprise, she saw Jason get up from under a pile of blankets.

Marie yelled, "Jason? What are you doing?"

Maxx heard her and said, "What, Jason's there! Tell him to go back."

Jason said to Marie, "I came to help you. I never get to do anything, and I thought that maybe, your job wasn't as dangerous as Marcos's, and so…I just want to help."

Marie looked at him with pity, "Jason, this is very dangerous."

Jason's eyes get teary.

Maxx said on the other line again, "Tell him to go back home. I have to go."

Marie looked at Jason and gave in, "Okay, you can come only if you stay safe and do exactly as I say."

Jason smiled, "Thanks, Marie."

Marie smiled and said, "Okay, let's get this over with."

They both get out of the vehicle.

Maxx put his phone down and looked out the window at the Pentagon building.

Ann looked out at it, "That's it."

Maxx parked his car two parking lots away from the building and got out.

Ann stepped out of the vehicle and asked, "So what's first?"

Maxx said, "First, we go through the sewers, and get inside that way."

He motioned for Ann to follow him, and he walked over to a grate in the ground. He lifted it up and hopped down inside.

Ann covered her nose and said, "Here it went."

Maxx poked his head out of the hole in the ground, "Here what went?"

"Oh, nothing just some dog went—"

"I thought it was something important." He interrupted, "Can you stay focused, Ann?"

"Oh, right of course," she said before following him into the sewers.

Pop was rushing through the hall of the FBI as Marian was saying, "One of our people spotted Marie. She's at SNOW. Should I make the drop on her?"

Pop sighed and looked at Marian, "By the way, Marian, you're fired. I have someone else I can use."

Marian was taken back, "What, who?"

Pop smiled and motioned for Marian to leave. Marian turned around with his head low. Pop got a phone call. He gasped and turned to Marian who was halfway out the door and said, "Marian, I unfired you! Go to the Pentagon. Maxx was spotted."

Marian had a leap of hope; he grabbed his coat and ran out.

Marie was inside her building, well, more like she was underneath it in the main control room.

Jason was a wiz on the computers. He shut down the security cameras and the electricity.

An alarm sounded, but Marie was not alarmed. She knew her agency building well. She simply turned off the alarms and headed upstairs to her office through the stairs.

Over at the Pentagon, Maxx and Ann were right underneath the main control room.

"It blew my mind that they didn't put security in the sewers." Ann whispered.

Maxx looked back at her with wide eyes as if he didn't know she was there this whole time.

She rolled her eyes and chuckled, "Not this again."

Maxx stopped and looked up through the grate. He held out his hand, "You have the USB?"

She handed it to him.

He added, "Also, do you have a bobby pin?"

Ann narrowed her eyes and got excited, "Yeah."

Maxx held out his hand expectantly. She reached up to her super-tight bun and took it out, letting the hair fall to her shoulders. She handed him the bobby pin. He took it and put it in his pocket.

He looked at her with her loose hair and nodded, "Much better."

Ann scoffed.

Maxx was back to business, "Here we are. Are you ready? As soon as we come out of the sewers, we expose ourselves and we have to act really fast."

Ann nodded, her heart pounding, "Let's do it."

Maxx nodded and climbed the moist stairs to the grate that led to the inside of the Pentagon.

1...2...3

He opened up the grate with a combination of speed and silence. Ann jumped up with him, and he put the gait back quickly. Immediately, he and Ann ran to the wall, and he spotted the security camera. He grabbed a high-voltage flashlight and quickly flashed it into the camera. As the camera started to malfunction, he and Ann ran through to the main control door. Within the same second, Maxx had the door unlocked with Ann's bobby pin as if it was as easy as opening the door itself.

They both ran into the room, and Maxx immediately ran up to the two men sitting at the computers.

He ran to them, and without breaking a sweat, he grabbed two white handkerchiefs and, with each hand, held them to their nose from behind them. Immediately, the two men went out without a struggle.

Ann just stood watching and thinking to herself, *Wow, he's actually doing everything.*

Once the men were knocked out, he motioned for her to come.

He gave her the key from one of the unctuous men and said, "Go to the next control room while I plug this USB into the main computer. You will get the information from these computers and then download it."

At that, Ann ran to the other door, opened it, and went inside.

Marie was up and, in her office, well almost to her office. She snuck down the hall when suddenly they heard a devilishly familiar voice, "Hold it there!" they both turned around and faced Pop and his gun.

He chuckled, "You thought I wouldn't know it if you guys snuck into my agency."

Marie put in, "It's my agency. I can do whatever I want with it."

Pop walked closer to them.

Marie pulled Jason behind her, "So what's next? You'll shoot us? You won't be able to explain it."

Pop laughed, "I don't need to explain it. Because soon M.A.X.X. operatives will be all over the planet, and I will have the whole world at my grasp. I control M.A.X.X. and Maxx. Little does he know, everything he does is being monitored. He was never lost to us; he was just quicker. But know, we are going to catch him, and when we do…"

Suddenly, a loud clang sounded from right behind Pop, and he dropped like a rock.

Marie looked at Pop on the ground in shock. And, behind him stood a girl who was about nineteen, and she was holding a frying pan, like Rapunzel.

Marie was confused, and she asked, "What? Who are you?"

The girl looked at her with frightened eyes, "I saw him run in after you into this building. I'm Tabitha, an old friend of Maxx. Don't worry. I know what you guys are up against."

Marie is skeptical, "How do you know that?"

Her face grew dark, "I was part of M.A.X.X. I escaped five years ago with Maxx."

Marie gasped. Maxx didn't escape alone.

Tabitha showed her a scar on her arm, "I was Number Fifty-Six."

Her arm revealed a scar in the exact shape of the number.

Marie gasped, "But how come Maxx didn't have that?"

Tabitha was silent but confident, "Maxx was the best that the agency ever had. They would never have done it to him. They were so confident in him, and look where it put them." She said that last part with amusement.

Marie could tell that the girl had been through a lot, she nodded her head, "We're going to my office."

Tabitha smiled at the thought of helping them.

She leaned down and tied up Pop with a bundle of rope that she brought.

"Ready."

The information was perfect and completely foolproof. It was all evidence that needed to put down M.A.X.X. for good.

All the data was together, and Maxx pressed the transfer into the USB that he had.

Ann said over the walkie-talkie, "I got it; it's downloading really fast."

Maxx quickly hooked the computer into the SNOW system, where Marie would be waiting.

After about a minute, Ann said excitedly, "Done. You ready?"

Maxx shook his head, "Ready."

The computer voice responded, "Data transfer complete."

He moved the arrow to the button that said, 'send'.

Suddenly, a voice yelled, "I wouldn't!"

Immediately Maxx had his gun out, and he wiped around to face Marion. But Marion had the advantage. He had Ann and was holding a knife to her throat.

Marion demanded, "Give me the USB."

Maxx almost kicked himself. He was caught, and the plan was about to fail.

He looked at Ann, "I told you to shout if anything happened."

Ann looked sad, "Sorry, I got caught up in the moment."

Marion demanded louder, "Put the gun down and take the USB out!"

Maxx slowly put the gun down and inched over to the other computer.

Marion warned, "Don't try anything funny."

"What are you talking about? I'm always funny." Maxx said before putting his hand on the computer and gently took the USB out.

Marion said, "Now give it to me."

Maxx looked at the USB and then at Marion; then he shrugged. He tossed the USB high in the air. It all happened within a split second. Marion let go of Ann and reach both his hand in the air to catch the USB.

Ann jumped for freedom, and Maxx lifted his gun again and shot. The scream that came from Marion was inhuman.

He fell to the ground, holding his leg, and said in amazement, "You shot me!"

He looked up at where Maxx was, but Maxx and Ann were gone.

You can imagine Marie's disappointment when the download did not work.

It said, 'Transfer incomplete. Unsuccessful'.

She sighed, "What happened?"

A deep voice answered, "Maybe they got caught."

Marie, Jason, and Tabitha all turned around. Pop had a big bruise on his head, and he held a gun at them, "Go to the roof. Now!" He ordered them out, waving his gun around in their faces. "You have no idea how much I'm going to enjoy this," Pop said as they walked in single file to the roof.

Immediately, they were all freezing in the ice-cold wind and blizzard-like conditions.

Outside was a very different climate. In fact, it was snowing so hard it was hard to see.

Pop had them all standing in a line facing him. He held the gun and looked at Tabitha, "I remember you. You escaped with Maxx." He smiled, "Well, you can join them at the bottom of the building."

Jason spoke up, shivering and teeth chattering, "You can't hurt us."

Pop just laughed and said, "Watch me." He lifted the gun that was in his hand or at least was in his hand. He gasped and searched for the gun that he literally had in his hand.

Tabitha suddenly lifted the gun at him and said in a firm, well-trained voice, "Don't move."

Pop sat still with wide eyes.

Marie was surprised that someone other than Maxx could do things beyond comprehension.

Tabitha ordered Pop to move closer to the edge of the building. Pop inched closer to the edge but then unexpectedly twirled around and grabbed Jason and held him to the edge, "Don't shoot, or I'll drop him."

Marie yelled, "No! Jason!"

Tabitha held firm with Pop's gun. Pop looked at her and knew he had the advantage. So did Marie and even Tabitha. But the one who knew it the most was Jason. He looked at the predicament. He knew Marie and Tabitha would let Pop go, for his life. But Jason had that stubborn part of him, the part that ran in his family. It was time for Pop to be brought down. Literally.

Just as Tabitha started to lower her gun, Jason looked at Pop and said, "If I die, you're coming with me."

Pop's face grew worried, but before he could react, Jason launched himself off the edge of the SNOW building, bringing Pop down with him.

The blood-curdling scream came from both Pop and Marie. Marie ran to the edge and sank to her knees crying and looking over the edge.

It was too snowy to see anything, but the cold was the last thing on her mind.

Marie wept bitterly, "Jason!"

Tabitha in the back dropped the gun and put her hands to her mouth to conceal her dropped jaw. Tears filled her eyes too. The snow was so blinding and white, and everything was suddenly quiet. Just the sound of the wind whistling through the city. The cold froze them both as they sat there in the foot-high snow.

Suddenly, Marie's phone rang. She wearily picked it up. Ann was on the other line.

Ann whispered to Marie, "Marie, I'm so sorry. We failed. The plan failed. Maxx and I are going to go immediately to plan B. I am not at liberty to tell you what it is because I don't know what it is, but Maxx said it was big!"

Marie got a sudden realization and determination. More than ever M.A.X.X. had to go, now.

She answered with determination, "I'll be over in less than ten minutes."

Ann seemed shocked by that, "What now?"

Marie said, "I have a way."

In Marie's garage, Marie and Tabitha jumped in a super intense, high-voltage electric racecar.

Tabitha was in awe, "You must be rich."

Marie ordered, "Buckle up."

Before Tabitha could, Marie sped out of there faster than a jet could have flown.

Maxx held the USB in his pocket. He had snatched it from the air when Marion was shot.

"Where are we going?" Ann asked.

Maxx was determined as he drove his car down the street, "First, I am going to turn the electricity out."

Ann looked wide-eyed. She knew what he meant. He wasn't going to just turn the electricity out in one building, but like before, he was going to make all the electricity go out over miles and miles.

Maxx screeched to a stop and ordered her to stay in the car. She folded her arms and huffed. Maxx hopped out of the car and shook his head at her attitude.

"Crazy girl," he mumbled before disappearing into the forest.

He had stopped at an electrical power plant. Taking this thing out could take out the whole state, but Maxx wasn't going to bomb it or anything. His special training helped him to know a thing or two about power plants.

He just had to cut a few important, wires, and power lines, and in case the repair people fix it too fast, then he would also turn off the emergency switch. No one would look at that when they were trying to fix a broken power line. It had its humor really.

He climbed up the fence with ease, and he simply ran toward the power lines. He looked up at them from the ground and produced a pair of rubber gloves and climbed the post.

He breathed deeply and counted in his head, *one...two...three...*and with speed, he grabbed the power line and pierced Ann's bobby pin all the way through it; at the same time, he leaped all the way back to the ground before the power line sent out a powerful shock. The pain of falling all that way was something Maxx was used to. But, this time, it was worse because his abdomen was still sore from the shot.

He ignored the loud crackling of the power line and the siren that sounded. He was across the next fence in no time, and next to the emergency off switch. He opened the glass with a yank and turned the off switch.

Onto the next thing…

Ann sat in her car fiddling with her phone when she heard the siren. She admired Maxx's handiwork happily. Then, right before her eyes, every light she saw everywhere was turned out. Within a few minutes, Maxx hopped into the driver's seat and said, "Onto the next step before M.A.X.X. finds out what we are doing."

Ann shrugged hoping he doesn't notice the flush in her cheeks, "What is next?" He did notice, but he paid no mind to it. He already knew he was awesome.

Maxx exhales as he sped out of the driveway, "Next, the Washington Monument. I have the USB, and I need to get it to Marie, but M.A.X.X. is on our trail. So I need to lead them somewhere they can't follow us."

Ann clued in, "We are going to lose them?"

Maxx nodded and winked at her, "It will be long enough, to get this USB Published, and viral. By then, it will be over."

Ann was excited and scared.

Marie was in her helicopter that she told her agent to prepare.

Tabitha was in the co-pilot's seat, "Be careful, Marie, we won't be able to do plan B if we die in a blizzard. Do you even know what plan B is?"

Marie exhaled but didn't answer.

She was thinking. *What could Maxx's plan B be? Think, Maxx. Maxx, what would he do? He would do something to get the USB to me, but M.A.X.X. will be all over him. He needed something. Think, Maxx, think…big?* She suddenly realized it. That had to be it. Was Maxx willing to try something that dangerous? She thought about it for a little bit, then decided, *Yeah, he was.* "We need to get to the top of the Washington Monument now!"

It was as if Marie had told her everything. Tabitha was on track in an instant, "It won't take him long to break the glass, trust me."

Marie nodded and rushed the helicopter over to the building.

Maxx and Ann were rushing faster than they had been before.

Ann was actually the first in the door. The lights were out, and there were plenty of shouting people. It was chaos; that was why no one stopped her when she ran to the elevator. She slapped the arrow up, button at least seven times.

"Come on." She was jumping up and down with adrenaline.

Maxx's voice hissed behind her in disbelief, "Oh, my gosh, what are you doing?"

She turned to him, "Trying to use the elevator." He shook his head franticly, "We don't use the elevator, ever! Plus, it does not work. No electricity. Look, Ann, I like you and all, but if this plan is going to work, we have to be on the same page, all right? My page!"

She nodded, then realized what that means, "We are going to walk up all those steps?"

Maxx had led her into the Stairway and handed her a flashlight. Ann looked up in amazement through the beam of the flashlight. The stairs never seemed to end.

Maxx was already on his way up and he had a quick, steady pace.

Ann struggled to keep pace. It seemed as though, one hour had passed.

Sweat drenched Ann's shirt, despite the cold weather outside. She couldn't even see the top of the steps yet. They just kept going. Finally, she collapsed in a dramatic flutter, "Go, Maxx. I can't make it. Go without me. I am done for."

She looked up and realized that Maxx was so much farther up the steps that she can barely see him.

She groaned and put her head down.

Suddenly, Maxx was there, and he was confused, as if he never knew someone could have such little stamina, "What are you doing now?"

She wheezed, "I can't go any further. My legs can't go another step, go without me."

Maxx rolled his eyes and even laughed a bit.

He said, "Pop and Marion and all the M.A.X.X. people are probably already on those steps down there. If you stay here, they will swarm you and you will die. And I can't let that happen! So you had better get up and keep going!"

Ann breathed in wheezy breathed, "I wish I had as much stamina as you, but I don't."

She exhaled again, as if her lungs were about to give away.

Maxx breathed and said under his breath, "Drama queen."

And with one, strong swoop, he picked her up like a puppy dog and went keeping the same pace as he had before. If not faster, to make up for lost time.

The top of the Washington Monument was a very elaborate room. It had fancy furnished chairs, pictures on the walls, and a view out of three windows.

Maxx put Ann down on a chair and said in a baby voice, "You think you can walk now, honey?"

Ann wrinkled her nose and mumbled thanks.

Maxx barely noticed because he was already next to the window, pounding it with his fists.

Ann was confused, she thought he would have a better plan than that, "That is four-inch ballistic glass. You will have to create more momentum." Ann informed him.

He stopped pounding and looked at her. He said dramatically, "I know, Ann."

He looked down and picked up a small hammer that happened to be in the corner. Probably from a construction crew yesterday. He lifted it to the glass and examined the glass closely as if he was about to do a great science project. And, with one hard bang, he smashed the hammer against the window and the whole thing and shattered.

Ann was jaw dropped, "That is impossible!"

Maxx narrowed his eyebrows and shrugged, "No it isn't. It is science."

Then a loud but wheezy voice demanded, "Step…(wheeze)…away from the…(wheeze)…window."

Maxx and Ann turned to face a group of men, and Marion was at the lead, wheezing and panting. His whole abdomen was in a cast already. As if he had broken a bone.

Maxx looked utterly defeated.

"Okay. Okay. You win. I give up." He took a step toward Marion, with his hands up. Then, without warning, He turned and grabbed Ann, and leaped out the window. Ann screamed as they disappeared completely.

All the men gasped. Marion was wide-eyed, "I was not expecting that."

He felt heroic, "Mission Accomplished, problem solved."

He turned around, then stopped when he heard a loud flapping outside.

"Do you guys hear that?" he turned around to the window and saw it. A huge helicopter flew into view. Marion's jaw dropped as he saw the four occupants. Marie was in the pilot's seat smiling, Tabitha was in the copilot's seat waving her hand, Maxx was in the back, busily on a computer with the USB, and Ann was still recovering from the shock of falling in the back. Then as quickly as they had appeared, they disappeared into the snow.

Marion jumped into action, "Fire at them! Take them down!"

All the men crowded to the window and fired at the helicopter, but Marie was already gone.

"Go downstairs! We have to stop them!"

Everyone rushed down the steps as fast as they could, but everyone knew that the Washington Monument was very, very tall.

Marie and Tabitha 'whooped' in the front.

Ann had recovered, "It is about time you guys came."

Marie defended herself, "I had to figure out Maxx's plan."

Ann turned her attention to Tabitha, "Who are you anyway?"

Tabitha reached her hand back, "I am Tabitha. I helped Maxx escape, all those years ago."

At the mention of Maxx's name, Maxx actually did not snap to attention. He was completely engulfed in the USB, "This thing had it all. This is it? All we have to do is send it in. This is enough evidence to take out everyone associated with M.A.X.X."

Then Maxx suddenly snapped to attention when he realized who was in the co-pilot's seat, "Wait a minute. Tabitha? What are you doing here?"

She seemed tense at Maxx's attention, "Um, I just wanted to help. I saw Marie at her SNOW castle, and I knew."

Maxx knew she was lying. He didn't know about what, but he did know something was up.

He looked down at his computer and typed some more. The USB was already connected, and it was ready to send.

He looked up again and noticed the tense mood between Tabitha and Marie.

"Marie? What do you want to tell me?"

She breathed in. If Maxx didn't know better, it was almost like a shaky breath, "Um, there is something you need to know."

Maxx nodded slowly and before Marie could say anything, Maxx's realization came down.

"Jason? What happened?" he looked at Marie searchingly.

Marie breathed and whispered as she landed the plane on the building of SNOW, "He pushed Pop off this building, and…he went down with him."

That hit Maxx like a bullet. He looked down at the computer and chuckled a silent sad one, "I always knew that somehow Jason would get his stupid head killed."

They landed the helicopter in silence. Ann started to cry. Maxx took his laptop and got out of the helicopter, without a word.

Marie looked at Tabitha and got out with Maxx and Ann.

"I am sorry. It is all my fault." Marie said in remorse as they were all in her office.

Maxx had set the open laptop on the desk without a word. His voice was steady as if he was trying not to let it shake, "Let's just finish this."

Marie said again, "It was all my fault."

Maxx finally snapped, "I wasn't your fault! It was mine! It was my fault five years ago when I finally let him help me take out M.A.X.X. I never should have given in, but I did. So let's just finish it. It is why he gave himself up. So this would be over. So help me; I am going to end it, hear and now!" With that said, he whipped out his gun, fast as lightning, and aimed it at Tabitha. Within the same second, Tabitha had her gun aimed at him.

Ann gasped at the sudden violence.

Marie narrowed her eyebrows, "What?"

Maxx and Tabitha had a bit of a staring contest, and then Tabitha said, "I didn't want to have to do this, but they threatened my family. I can't let you download that USB. I won't."

Maxx was adamant, and Tabitha knew him well. He wasn't going to just give up. She suddenly aims the gun at Ann.

Marie gasped and Ann gasped, "Why am I always the victim?" she whispered to herself.

Tabitha demanded with a shaky voice, "Pass the USB over gently, or she dies."

Maxx was still adamant, "And let my brother die for nothing. You can just go jump in a lake." Tabitha narrowed her eyebrows, "You think I won't shoot? I will! I will for my family."

Maxx finally seemed reluctant, "Okay, fine."

He took the USB and slowly stepped closer to her, handing it to her.

She took it and pointed the gun at him again. She stepped back toward the door, "They also told me to get rid of you. Their words were, 'Because you were a pain to the whole organization'. It isn't anything personal, Maxx. We were a great team back in the day, but I went on to make a family and have a life. But you just couldn't walk away. You have always been tied to this organization. You never could just leave it alone. You had to keep looking back and look where it got you—look where it got Jason. I have a family Maxx, who do you have?"

Those last words have been jumbling around in his head since the beginning. Who did he have? Such small words could have a great impact on a person like him.

Maxx looked serious when suddenly Ann steps up, "He has me!"

Maxx looked shocked for a second but dived right in. he smiled a little bit at Tabitha, "Yeah, that's right."

Marie was wide-eyed in the background. She steps in, "Woah woah! Is there something that I should know?" she looked at Maxx and Ann.

"Yeah! Your blind!" Tabetha said annoyed.

Ann was standing next to Maxx, and Maxx had his arm around her shoulder.

Marie was thoroughly confused, "When did this happen?"

Maxx and Ann both have blank stares. They shrugged at the same time.

Marie was taking this in, as was Tabitha. In Tabitha's eyes, Maxx was never an emotional person.

Marie finally smiled, "Actually, I think you two are so cute for each other."

Ann groaned while Maxx looked shocked that Marie would say such a thing.

Immediately Maxx let go of Ann and said, "How could you say that, Marie? We are not cute! Ew! That is so the wrong wording. I would say more…perfect."

Marie's eyes widened, "Really?"

Maxx thought about his words and changed them, "No. Not like that. I mean individually. Not together, I mean individually perfect. She is perfect."

Ann gasped, horrified. She butted in, "That is not true. He is the perfect one."

Maxx was thrown off guard by that. He looked at her with a confused expression, "Uh, no. we talked about this, remember?"

Ann was getting worked up, "Yes! We talked about it and it was you…"

Maxx interrupted, "I am perfect, you are right. Ed Sheerin clearly said that 'she' looked perfect tonight. Not 'he'! 'She'! Plus, I don't wear dresses!"

By this time Marie just had a weirded-out facial expression. She looked at Tabitha and motioned for her to intervene.

Tabitha was confused when she finally held the gun up again.

Tabitha, "Shut up! This is weird and wrong, and it ends now!"

And, without any more words, she pulled the trigger. Ann and Marie screamed, "No!"

The shot must have been so loud; it made everyone go deaf because they didn't even hear anything.

Ann and Marie were squeezing their eyes shut.

Ann was crying, but why hadn't she heard anything?

They both open their eyes and see it. Maxx was still standing straight, and so was Tabitha. In fact, all that was heard was a click.

Tabitha narrowed her eyebrows, and she started breathing harder, for fear.

"What? No!" she opened the clip of the gun and found exactly what made her scared, there were no bullets. A clang sounded in everyone's ears. They looked at Maxx. He smiled smugly and held out his balled-up fist, he opened it. Out fell about seven bullets onto the floor.

Tabitha's eyes were wide. Maxx whipped out his gun again and shot at her leg.

She yelped and grasped her leg. She looked up at him, "Please...I...I have a family."

Maxx stopped, "I know, that is why I am letting you live. Besides, about that USB, you can keep it." Tabitha's eyes narrow. Maxx looked confused and asked, "I wonder what the forecast is today. Light showers? Slight chance of rain. Marie, would you mind turning on the news?"

Everyone seemed confused, but Marie stepped to the TV in the corner and turned it on. The image that flashed made everyone gasped, except Maxx.

On the TV, it showed the building they were in, being surrounded by police officers. And a small video in the corner showed Marian and his men in handcuffs being hauled away.

Maxx looked back at Tabitha and smiled brightly, "Oh. It actually looks pretty sunny. I already sent the information when Marian got shot. I figured, if the plan went wrong so fast, then it was too unstable to wait. So that is when I went to that power plant. Secretly, of course, I plugged in the USB to the power hard drive. As soon as the electricity turned back on, boom! You were all exposed. So keep the USB; it is empty after all. It is over. They already picked up Marion and his crew at the Washington Monument…still on the stairs."

Tabitha was wide-eyed as 'they' all hear a lot of footsteps outside the door.

Maxx wheeled to Marie and flashed his famous smile. Marie smiled and asked, "By the way. All that Lovey-dovey thing with you and Ann was an act, right? To distract everyone for the cops to get here, right?" Maxx looked at her, hesitates a second, then shrugged, "Yeah, of course." He looked at Ann.

She nervously shook it off, "Duh."

Then Maxx was back to business. He turned to Marie giving her his gun, "Don't tell them who we are."

He motioned for Ann to follow him, and they ran to the other room.

Marie looked after them; they were both gone. She knew that they were both lying about the 'act', but she did not probe. It was none of her business.

The police burst through the door and found Tabitha hurt, Tabitha the one who was still part of M.A.X.X., and Marie, the one who saved the day.

Chapter Eighteen

Friday, December 11, 2042

"Good morning, New York City. This is Steve Armstrong, recently promoted to CNN national television. I am here today with none other than Marisa Willis for some more alarming news. Hang on folks, you might want to take a seat. Marisa?"

"Thanks, Steve, and hello, New York. I am happy as well for the promotion, but today isn't about me; there has been a development. Just after the power grid was restored by highly trained repairmen, every electronic in this state and all states surrounding, and the world, burst to life with one thing on their screen, M.A.X.X. that is right folks, you heard me. The long thought abandoned illegal organization, M.A.X.X. was just found out to be fully functioning. The electronics showing this information were literally showing all kinds of information. It had the leaders; it had the children's occupants. It had the location of all the districts. Millions of arrests have been made all over the world, starting with judges, lawyers, teachers, doctors, and even the president of the United States.

"The one behind the blackout was found to be the one who sent out this information. It was found out recently that

one very brave young woman, Marie Winterfield, was the one behind the exposure of M.A.X.X. Marie is the head of her own SNOW agency, and since she had been kicked out by an FBI agent, she decided to look into it, by herself, that is when she found out it was M.A.X.X. and she spent weeks trying to expose them. The very generous woman that she is, Marie, actually quit her job, to join a rehabilitation orphanage where all the kids who were stolen by M.A.X.X. were transferred. Even after all this, she is still saving lives, trying to fix what M.A.X.X. has destroyed.

"Marie was adamant that two individuals fell off her roof in the struggle. One, Pop, otherwise known as Percy Owens Peterson, founder of M.A.X.X., and the other, a young boy Jason Plumer who was responsible for Percy's fall. And, though, Peterson's body has been recovered, Plumber's body is yet to be found.

"But that is not all folks; there are two individuals that are out in the streets. One of them being the most dangerous and skilled of the whole M.A.X.X. organization. They have not been found yet and are still at large. They are very dangerous, criminals of the law. The girl that is on the run is the known sister of the leader of M.A.X.X. Marion Cogsdale, who was arrested earlier today. Locals believe that she is working to relive her brother's legacy, and the man she is with is the one you have to watch out for folks. They say that he is the mastermind of the whole thing, and he doesn't have to be armed to do some harm...See what I did there? His name is...Maxx."

Marie Winterfield walked down the sidewalk in the snow.

The sky was white with clouds and thick flurries. It had been two weeks since she had seen the hide or hair of Maxx or Ann. They had gone under the radar, while she had become famous.

Something inside her wanted to shout from the rooftops that Maxx and Ann were innocent. That it wasn't her who saved the kids, it was Maxx, but the last thing Maxx had told her was to never tell them who they were.

She stood still; her nose was bright red in the cold.

"Makes you want to fall to the ground and make a snow angel."

She turned her head around to the familiar voice. Not four feet away, Maxx stood there gazing at the sky. He had a hood that covered most of his head. He looked at Marie and smiled.

Marie gasped, "Maxx, what are you doing here? You can't be out in the open. You could get caught!" Maxx looked at her seriously. She looked down. Okay, he wouldn't get caught, she knew that.

"Why did you come?" she asked as she looked at him.

He smiled and looked at the sky again, "I just wanted to thank you. You did more to help me than most people would have. And I will always be grateful. I just wanted you to know that. I couldn't have done it without you." She smiled and was about to say, welcome, when Maxx changes his words quickly, "I mean, I could have done it without you, but that would have been much too easy. It would have involved technology wipeouts, chemistry, physiology, niacin, benzodiazepine, trigonometry, denatonium benzoate, you don't even want to know what else."

Marie laughed with glee. She should have known. Maxx always did try things the hardest way first, "You are welcome, Maxx. I don't think I would have been able to join the rehabilitation orphanage if you hadn't chosen me."

She adds on with interest, "How is Ann? Or is it classified?"

Maxx gave her a mischievous grin and said, "Tell you what. We will visit you at that rehabilitation place when things calm down."

Marie gets sad suddenly, "This will never calm down. It's the biggest thing since the atomic bomb and Pearl Harbor."

Maxx nodded his head slowly then said quietly, "It will. Someday when people realize that it is over, they will move on. But if you are really worried about Ann, then I will make a deal with you. If anything, bad almost happens to her under my supervision, then I will give up and send her to you."

Marie laughed out loud. That was a trick because if Maxx couldn't protect her, no one could, right?

But she said, "Deal."

He nodded, "One more thing…call me Marcos. I am not Maxx anymore."

She turned to look at him, but he was gone. Vanished. She could have sworn she heard a silent, "Goodbye, Marie." But it was so subtle, that it could just as easily have been the wind whistling through the streets. She did not bother to look for him, that would be a waste of time. She smiled. Maxx was the strangest person she had ever met, but she was glad she had met him. Because even though things were very difficult, scary, confusing, sad, or downright infuriating sometimes, everything did work out in the end. And they were all stronger because of it.

Epilogue

"That is where we will end our story," Marie said with a smile.

"What? Is that the end?"

"Jason died!"

"Marcos was funny. He-he."

The kids at the rehabilitation orphanage were all laughing.

Thirty-eight-year-old Marie smiled and said calmly, "Now off to bed. Tomorrow morning is Christmas."

All the kids cheered.

Marie calmed them down by waving her hands, "That is the end of our story kids. You know the drill."

In the background, the janitor was mopping. He was in an orange Community Service Suit. He had been intrigued by the story, and he had sat down to listen. This janitor was actually Marion Cogsdale.

One little girl said, "Miss Winterfield? What happened to Marcos and Ann?"

All the kids were silent.

Marie looked up and said, "Well, wouldn't you like to know?"

But then she is interrupted by a huge thud. Suddenly, ash and soot fly everywhere. They all heard coughing and a deep voice saying, "That wasn't really a good idea."

Suddenly, out of the ashes, belly first, came a guy dressed up as Santa Claus.

He regained his composure and did a hearty "Ho, Ho, Ho!"

All the kids cheered and ran toward him, "Yeah!"

Marie whispered to Marian, "Who is that?"

Marian was furious, "I don't know, but I am not cleaning that up!"

Santa sat down and slapped his knee, indicating for a child to come sit on his lap, "What do you want for Christmas, Lassie?"

One little girl said, "I want a puppy."

Santa looked at Marie, and she said, "Uh, I don't think that's a good idea."

All the kids nodded their heads in agreement. The little girl started to cry, and suddenly, Santa lost it. He yelled in a very familiar voice, "Oh, just give the darn kid a puppy!"

Then he reached under his big belly and wiped out a great big Sant Bernard dog.

The girl gasped, "I got a puppy!"

Marie noticed though that Santa was not fat anymore.

Then an older kid walked up to Santa and said, "I know what I want."

Then the kid pulled Santa's beard off, and all the kids gasped. The man behind the beard was Marcos!

All the kids yelled, "Marcos!"

Marie gasped and screamed with the kids, "Marcos!"

Marcos shrugged and said, "What's the use for disguises anymore."

He ripped the Santa clothes off, revealing a nice red and green, wool Christmas Jacket and yelled, "Yep, it's me! Merry Christmas kids!"

Marian gasped and pulled his phone out, fumbling with it before dialing 911, "Hello? I have an emergency!"

The phone slipped out of Marian's hand, and he looked to see Ann holding it.

"Hi, big bro! Miss me?" then she dropped the phone on the ground and smashed it with her high, high heels.

Then Marie spotted Ann. Ann yelled, "Surprise!"

All the kids yelled louder. On her side, Ann was holding a little toddler boy, and standing next to them was a little girl.

Marie gasped and ran to Ann, "Oh, my gosh. Ann, you never told me."

Ann was smiling big, "Marie, this is little Maxx."

Marcos burst in and gestured to their daughter saying, "Yes, and we named this little one after her uncle."

At that, Marion looked up and was intrigued, "After me?"

Marcos nodded and flashed his famous smile, "Yep, her name's Mary Ann."

Marion clenched his fists and jaws and took a deep breath.

In.

Out.

In.

Then he smiled and forced out a hardy laugh. Then Marie finally let out a laugh, and Marcos, Ann, and all the kids.

Marcos stopped abruptly and listened. Sirens were heard in the distance. Everyone was silent. Marcos peeked out the window and saw an army of vehicles coming their way, but strangely, they weren't cop cars.

One little girl walked up to Marcos, "Are you going to have to leave?"

He leaned down to her and said, "I am going to leave, yes. But at least I got to see you all. You guys seem like you are doing much better. I am very proud. I have to get out of here now."

The sirens were getting closer. Marcos went up to Ann quickly and gave her a quick hug, "See you at the rendezvous? And careful with these people; whoever they are, they aren't cops."

Ann nodded, not worried at all. Marcos tussled his boy Maxx's hair and kissed his girl Mary Ann on the cheek, "See you guys later. Daddy has got to run."

He turned to Marie, Marion, and all the kids, "Bye, guys." Marie smiled and waved.

She turned to Ann quickly, "You don't have to go?"

Ann shook her head, "Maxx…I mean, Marcos, was able to arrange something. They all know that I am innocent. And, if they question me too much about where he is, I can sue and win. They are still looking for him, but I am safe, and so is he."

Marie nodded as Marcos stopped for a brief second, looking back at the windows, a little worried; then he disappeared into the bathroom.

The cars are outside, and the building is surrounded.

But nobody paid attention. One boy ran closer to the restroom, and everyone heard a toilet flush.

The boy yelled in a babyish voice, "He's gone!"

THE END